DARK SOUL

Guardians of the Fae Realms: Book 7
JL Madore

Dark Soul: Guardians of the Fae Realms

JL Madore -- 1st ed.

ISBN: 978-1-998372-64-5

AUTHOR NOTE

Dark Soul is the second book in Nakeyla's harem and book 7 in The Guardians of the Fae Realms.

If you missed the first harem and the intro to how we got here, start at book 1 of the entire series as this story is a continuation of plot and cast of character from the first group of lovers. Guardians of the Phoenix.

If you started with Dark Curse, book one of this trilogy, that's fine too.

Enjoy,

JL

CHAPTER ONE

Creed

The contact of skin-to-skin thrums like a jolt of electricity from the ink of our joined mating marks. The energy throbs through my pounding heart, and straight to my aching cock. Technically, Keyla's hand in mine is no longer a necessity of life or death, but I grew fond of it over the past three days and am not willing to give it up.

I'm not sure if it's the same for her, but she doesn't hesitate to lace our fingers when I prompt her to hold my hand, so I choose to think that's telling. "Do you feel it, Little Wolf? Destiny is calling."

She smiles up at me as we make our way through the crush of civilians outside the portal hub. Her brown eyes are as dark and rich as Travon chocolate and hold more trust and compassion than I deserve. "I do."

"Is your destiny beacon back?" Dillan asks.

Keyla shifts her attention to the third in our mating, the ex-military bear shifter she was in love with when the universe soul-seared us as the perfect match for one another. I consider him her plus one, but she wants us to be more than that.

Who knows? Maybe we will be.

"Yes, it's back," she says, as we reach the stairs into the building and start climbing. "It subsided when we first arrived in Dornte but disappeared after the mating. It's back now and it's calling."

"I remember that feeling," Kotah says, jogging along beside us. "As uncertain as things seemed then, it led me to a life I never dreamed possible."

I cast a sideways glance and meet the Wolf King's easy smile. Can anyone be this nice? Kotah has been nothing but understanding and supportive since this whole mating mess began.

It makes sense he wants Keyla to be happy and safe, but even when I scan his mental energies and intentions, with my mind guardian gifts, he genuinely wants the best for me as well.

How is that possible? He doesn't know me.

As crazy as it sounds, sometimes I swear simply being near him makes me feel calmer and more at peace with the mess that is my life.

We crest the top step of the Dornte portal hub and as citizens recognize me, they shift out of our way and bow. Kotah and Keyla smile as we pass and genuinely acknowledge them. I realize, in many ways, I've never embraced being set apart as their prince.

In my youth, I tried to blend in, work alongside the citizens, learn about their lives, and show them I was one of them. The past two years since my father was killed and my crown was taken, I learned how wrong I was.

I'm either their prince or I'm not.

And if I'm their prince, I need to fight for the throne of the quadrant I'm destined to rule. Keyla said her brother, Kotah, never wanted to become King of the Human Realm but when their father died last week, the male straightened up and assumed his place.

It's hard to believe he's only been a king for a week.

Watching them interact with my citizens is humbling. They aren't stopping or speaking with them, and yet, even the way they hold their heads and nod makes it obvious they are more 'royal' than I am.

They are gracious and warm.

They seem to value the people around them whether they are attendants in the portal gate or displaced citizens living in the tunnels below the city or strangers smiling at them on the street.

They make it look easy.

Keyla said I have the right to be guarded after years of torment and torture and that's true, but it's not the kind of king I want to be once we reclaim my throne.

"Everything all right?" Keyla asks, squeezing my hand. We've entered the main atrium at the Dornte portal hub, and a hundred people are shuffling around us.

I lean in and kiss her cheek. "Fine. Just adjusting to my new world."

"And are they welcome adjustments?"

I take in our group: my stunning wolf queen, our broody but intelligent bear, my brother-in-law Wolf King, and my... Rhylan.

Rhylan isn't *my* anything. At least not anymore.

I meet Rhy's scowl, and it gives me a sour taste in my mouth. His foul disposition is nothing new, but something changed. This anger is directed at me.

Is he mad I'm wriggling out from under his thumb? Does he resent the first spark of happiness and hope I've had in over two years? Did he expect me to remain a prisoner in my wing of my own castle for the rest of my life? In truth, it's me who should be furious.

He held me prisoner.

He lied about my mother's death.

He has no right to be angry with me.

Keyla presses a hand to my cheek and recaptures my full attention. "My prince?"

I blink and snap back to the moment at hand. "Yes, sorry, what? Oh, apologies, you asked me something."

Her gaze is intimate and unarming. I've spent the past two years locking myself away from the world and it's unsettling to have someone slip under my defenses as easily as Keyla does. "I wondered if the adjustments to your world are welcome. Are you all right?"

I stop and our group slows to stop around us. Lifting her chin with my finger, I bend to capture her lips. Whatever this is —the soul-searing or our mating bond or simply the blessing of having a female devoted to me and a brighter future in sight—it is bliss to kiss her.

Magic.

I claim her mouth and the primal growl of her wolf rumbles in my chest. My body responds immediately. Her mind is strong and the depth of her desire hits me on a level I've never experienced with anyone before now.

My cock hardens, ready to sate her.

She nips at my lip and then pushes her tongue between the seam, demanding access to my mouth. She's aggressive and playful, my mate. My heart skips a beat and then slows, a balmy rush blooming all over my skin.

Sadly, this is neither the time nor the place.

Easing back from the kiss, I swallow, a little embarrassed that I'm as hard as a steel rod while out in public. Still, she asked me a question. "Yes, very welcome... and more than a little overwhelming."

The way she bites her bottom lip doesn't help.

I want to be somewhere private and bite that lip too.

Something in the air shifts and when I straighten, I realize the crush of the crowd closest to us is holding up their datapads, snapping photos, and taking videos.

I straighten, pulling Keyla to my side.

Kotah chuckles. "You are their prince. The way into their hearts is by allowing them into yours."

"Now is not the time," Rhylan hisses. "Queen Laryssa won't appreciate a public scene."

Queen Laryssa can go fuck herself.

I consider my options and decide to lead by the Northwood example. "Good morning, everyone. I have news and since I seem to have caught your attention, why wait? You may have heard rumors the phoenix has risen. I can confirm those rumors are true. Three days ago, the prophecy was realized and Calliope Tannis and her guardians opened a rift to the Human Realm."

There's a great gasp of excitement and I hold up my hand to continue. "Queen Laryssa and I ventured to the other realm to make contact and while many details still need clarification before we consider public travel, King Nakotah Northwood of the Human Realm is here as my guest to establish access to the four quadrants."

I gesture to Kotah and he stands tall and greets my citizens with a wave.

"And on a personal note," I say, wrapping my arm around Keyla and reaching to squeeze Doc's shoulder. "The universe stepped in to solidify the uniting of the two realms. The moment I locked eyes with this beautiful female, we were soul-seared. May I introduce Princess Nakeyla Northwood and her wildling mate Dillan Baskins."

The mixed excitement and confusion over that are expected, but I figure it's better to address our trio head-on rather than let them speculate.

"The universe gave the phoenix her quint to lead her to great things, I too have been blessed with multiple mates as well. I understand it is unusual, but more common in the Human Realm. And really, who are we to argue with the will of the fae universe?"

I lift my branded palm for them to take a few pictures and Keyla does the same. Another surge of excitement washes through the crowd.

With that taken care of, I refocus on the buzz burning in my skull. "Now, if you'll excuse us, we have a great many matters to attend to. I'll be sure to keep you posted as developments arise. Blessed be."

The crowd takes a few more photos but when they realize they aren't going to get anything more from me, they shuffle off and return to their initial reasons for being here.

"Nicely done," Kotah says, smiling. "You've captivated their curiosity while also upstaging Laryssa and taking away her opportunity to make this about her."

Rhylan grunts. "And you'll pay for it. That was stupid and you know it."

"No, it wasn't." Keyla hugs my arm and grins. "It would've been stupid to allow Laryssa to claim something that wasn't hers to claim."

I sigh. "Rhylan is right, though. There is always a cost when Laryssa doesn't get what she wants."

Keyla's gaze narrows on me. "We won't let her take it out on you. Everything you said was true."

Doc frowns. "Except for a little blurring of the line when it came to the princess and her wildling mate."

I lift my shoulder. "They don't need to know the timing of your bonding. The point is, we're in it together now and I've claimed you both in public, so there's not much Laryssa can do about it."

Rhy rolls his eyes at me, but regardless of what he thinks, I'm done being Laryssa's whipping boy.

With our privacy returned to us, I scan the vast atrium of the portal hub. "Why do you think the beacon drew us here?"

"Maybe you need to travel to one of the other quadrants," Doc suggests.

Rhy growls. "Another quadrant is out of the question. There's no way we can swing that. Not happening."

My gaze locks on a woman on the opposite end of the station. The conversation around me is drowned out by the sudden thundering of blood rushing to my head. "I know why we're here."

Pulled by a strength of hatred I've never felt before, I track the red-haired beauty through the crowd and move to intercept. There may be a hundred people and two hundred feet between us, but they don't register.

There is just her and me.

Rhy curses somewhere close by. "Slecking hell. Don't Creed. Not her. Not here."

Keyla is jogging beside me, my strides cutting the distance between me and my target.

The woman enters the gate station for Clarinta, and now I'm the one jogging.

"What's happening? Who is she?" Keyla asks.

"That's the woman who cursed me and is stealing my soul with her dark beast. That's the blood witch."

Keyla

I rush across the polished floor of the Dornte portal station with my two mates, my brother, and Creed's prison guard—and super-secret-sex-partner—Rhylan. Scanning the sea of bodies, I telegraph Creed's gaze and find a stunning woman with a curvaceous body and scarlet hair.

"That's the blood witch that cursed you?" I say, the weight of that sinking in. "You're sure?"

Creed glances back at me and the hair on the ruff of my neck stands on end. "I'm sure. When someone looks you in the eye while they infect you with a soul-sucking demon beast, you commit their face to memory."

Well, all righty then.

He strides off and the four of us fall in line.

"I'm not saying we let her get away," Doc says, sidestepping between two men in uniform, "but do you think it's wise to confront her in a place packed wall-to-wall with innocent civilians?"

Creed slows his pace a little.

The woman hasn't seemed to notice us, and the fifty people between us and her are likely keeping our presence concealed. For the moment at least.

As the flow of traffic makes its way to the portal gate leading to Clarinta, Doc's concern gains weight. Do we want to start a battle of magic and murderous intent in the middle of a public transport site?

"What if we follow her and see where she's going?" I suggest. "If the beacon pulsing within us brought us to her, you're meant to have your moment. Only maybe it's not at the expense of the safety of your citizens."

He winces and then curses. The logic of the situation seems to get through the cloud of betrayal and fury shadowing him but he's not happy about it.

"We can't follow her to Clarinta," Rhy snaps. "Laryssa will lose her mind. I can't allow that."

"What makes you think I need your permission?" Creed snaps, turning on him.

Rhylan stiffens. "Don't make me be a dick, Creed."

Kotah sets a hand on Rhy's arm and I feel the pulse of his omega gift flow. "We'll say I needed to reach out to the leaders of the other quadrant to begin preparations to connect them to the other realm. For the moment, she's unsure how to challenge my presence."

"For the time being, we can use that to our advantage," Doc says, agreeing. "Laryssa knows coming straight at an enemy before you gauge what you're in for isn't the best strategy."

We arrive at the passageway to access the other quadrant and despite Rhylan's protest, Creed doesn't slow down. He has no intention of remaining in Dornte.

That is… until Rhylan rushes him and pushes up in front of him. "You're not going."

"You're wrong." Creed narrows his gaze and I feel the surge of power at the same time Rhy crumples to the ground clutching his head.

I'm torn. My place is with Creed, but I can't simply leave the man doubled over in the middle of the portal station with his nose bleeding.

What if Creed's done real damage?

He'll regret that later.

"You go," Kotah says, reading my struggle. "I'll help the dragon, and we'll be right behind you."

Doc takes my hand and the two of us run to catch up with my very pissed-off prince.

CHAPTER TWO

Doc

$\mathcal{I}$ have a feeling a life mated to these two won't be dull. As we leave the dragon tugging his shirt up to catch the blood gushing from his nose, I wonder how much damage a mind guardian fae can do?

I'm not sure what the universe has in store for Keyla but she won't face it alone. Even if I don't trust her fated mate, he opened the door for me to protect her and that's what I'll do... even if it's from him.

Keyla and I may have only mated a few hours ago, but in my heart and to my bear, she's been my mate from the beginning.

With a hand on the small of her back, we follow close on Creed's tail. We're only ten feet behind him as he passes through the golden glow of what looks like a simple archway of light.

We don't break stride and almost immediately emerge on the other side. Although the scenery has changed, little else has. Creed's still ten feet in front of us following the red-haired witch thirty feet farther ahead of him.

Keyla looks at me and smiles. "That was much better than our first trip through a portal gate."

I nod. "These people have obviously got their bridges established properly. Don't worry, Hawk and Lukas will get ours up and running."

"I hope it's soon." She puts a little extra hustle on to catch up to her prince. The speed puts an extra bit of sway into her breasts and I admit, I'm not complaining.

The sounds of the travelers moving through the portal station echo off the blue and ivory marble walls. We step into the atrium and honestly, it seems a hell of a lot friendlier than the one we just left.

Keyla hustles her sweet little ass to catch up with the silver-haired prince and reaches to retake her place at his side. The moment her palm slides against his, some of the tension drains out of his frame.

I know how he feels.

Kotah may be the omega and the one born with the calming power but Keyla soothes my soul the same way.

When we exit the portal station, it takes a moment to orient my senses. The air smells like cinnamon and where the buildings in Dornte were steel and stone, like most cities, this one has pastel-colored buildings in a rainbow of uplifting colors.

It's like we stepped out of a metropolis and ended up in a painting of a seaside escape.

"This city is so cute," Keyla says.

I'm not surprised she thinks so. It exudes positive energy.

"Dornte isn't at its best with Laryssa in charge," Creed snaps.

My bear lets off a rumble. "Easy. No need to take your shit out on Keyla."

Keyla meets my gaze and shakes her head. "It's fine. My comment wasn't meant as an insult to his quadrant, but emotions are running high."

"He still doesn't get to snap at you."

"And you don't get to growl at him on my behalf. He's my mate as you are. I won't have you defending me against him. We're a team now. We are three."

That's a bit of a sucker punch to the balls, but yeah, I've been told.

Creed turns quickly and grabs Keyla around the waist. Spinning her behind the column of a glass awning, he pulls her from the stream of commuters waiting for a shuttle by the street.

As before, the moment he claims her mouth, she melts against his muscled frame. The sudden PDA catches me off guard, but she doesn't put up an ounce of protest. Does she trust him so implicitly that she's at ease with him manhandling her like that?

I rein in my bear's protective response and look at the situation with a wider lens. The blood witch is hailing a car and scanning the area.

Keyla's wolf lets off a playful growl as he amps up the kiss from an act of distraction to diving down her throat with his tongue to see if she still has her tonsils.

When her arousal hits me, I expect to lose my mind. Tightening my hold on my bear, I lock down and await the rush of testosterone and possession.

Instead, my cock weighs in and decides the two of them macking like horny teenagers is fucking hot.

"Your witch is getting away," I say, my voice husky and deep. "If you're still interested."

"Fuck," Creed says, pulling back and looking dazed. "Where? What conveyance is she in?"

Kotah and Rhylan arrive as I raise my hand and point. "That blue and silver car at the intersection. The one with its indicator on to go left."

"Shit, we'll never catch it."

∾

Keyla

"Kotah and I might be able to run it down?" I offer, catching my breath. What started as a ruse to disguise our presence quickly got away from us and now, because we were unable to fight the attraction building between us, the key to Creed's curse is driving away.

Creed shakes his head and turns with a pleading gaze. "I know I probably don't deserve your help but—"

"You absolutely don't," Rhy snaps, his golden gaze feral with fury. "You're a slecking asshole and I have a massive headache now, you prick."

"Please, Rhy. You can hate me later. Please."

Rhylan is still grumbling as he takes a few running steps and launches into the mid-afternoon sky. His body explodes in the air and what was a man a moment ago bursts into a scaled dragon a split-second later.

As difficult as he and his twin can be, seeing their dragons in flight is breathtaking.

"So, you blow up your prison guard's brain cells and he does you the solid of chasing down the witch bitch who works for his boss?" Doc cants his head sideways and narrows his gaze. "What am I missing?"

Creed ignores his question and presses his hand against the panel of a metal podium near the street. The screen lets off a beep and then a light on the top of the stand flashes green.

The moment a car stops, Creed taps the screen again and the four of us get in. My prince slides into the driver's seat with Kotah in the front and Doc and I jump into the back.

The navigation screen of the car beeps as Creed taps his way through commands and adjusts the settings. "Release auto-drive. Manual control override."

"Releasing auto-drive is unadvised," an automated voice says through the speakers.

"Understood. Do it anyway." The automated car lady drones on for a bit about the safety benefits of the auto-drive system, but Creed is already pulling away from the curb. "Someone find Rhylan in the sky and tell me where I'm going."

Kotah is leaning forward, looking out the front windshield. Doc and I search the side windows. Wow, the sky is littered with traffic. As strange as it seems, many fae in this realm have wings.

"I've got him," Doc says. "On the left. Ten o'clock. Take the next turn if you can."

I'm leaning to the side, bending low to look up through Doc's window when he starts chuckling. He adjusts me as I hover over his lap and winks. "While you're down there... if you're bored."

I laugh, amazed at how much has changed in twenty-four hours. Yesterday at this time I was screaming and being raced to Creed's suite. Now I'm mated to both of them, and we can laugh about it.

At least a little.

"There, I've got him," Kotah says, pointing. "It looks like he's readying to land on that purple building."

We drive along for a little longer and then Creed pulls the vehicle to the side of the street. We all lean to look out our windows to get the lay of the land.

Growing up, I always pictured StoneHaven and the Fae Realm as being a dark, war-torn place with rubble and suffering. Clarinta blows my mind.

It's quaint and bright and judging by the dozens of different fae out in the open, it's inclusive. Add that to the air smelling like Cinnabon and it's a deliciously delightful place.

And still, for all the differences, the foundation of society remains much the same. They have buildings and cars and pedestrians and it's all very familiar.

"Engage auto-drive," Creed says, tapping the screen to close our use of the car. "Rental complete."

"Peace and happiness be with you," the automated car lady says.

"To you as well," I say, getting out.

Creed looks at me and blinks. "You realize that's an automated recording, right?"

I nod. "I'm not sure if you have AI sci-fi movies in this realm, but in our realm, it's common knowledge that one day the computers will get fed up with humanity treating them badly and will rise in revolt and take over the world. Might as well make a few friends with the other side while we can."

He laughs. "You're amazingly ridiculous for an educated female."

"Um... thank you?"

~

Rhylan

Creed and his mates will get me killed. At this rate, it's not a question of *if* it's *when*. There's no way in hell he should be in Clarinta and if he confronts the blood witch and it gets back to Queen Laryssa, what do I say? I have a soft heart and a solid cock? That my masochistic need to fuck the wrong person made me do it?

The midday sun warms the scales on my back, and I track the redhead into a thirty-story building. Descending for a landing, I angle to set down on the roof.

It won't matter why I let it happen. Laryssa will have me and Vik killed simply *because* it happened. Sure, I could out Creed and say he mind-fucked me *again* and left me on the ground.

I think that hurts worse than the fear of Vik and I paying the ultimate price. That's twice this week he's used his mind guardian gift against me.

Slecking asshole.

A city rental vehicle pulls to the curb on the street below and I try to rein it in. I'm an idiot. I should fly down there, pick him up in my talons, and fly his ass back to the portal station. That makes the most sense.

So why aren't I doing it?

Because the shit between me and Creed has never made sense... to me anyway.

When the four of them are out of the car and standing on the walkway in front of the building, I step over the edge and drop to the street below. The wind feels good against my scales and I extend my thirty-foot wingspan before I reach the ground to slow my descent.

Touching down with Creed and his new mates, I give my wings a flap and push them with a gust of air.

Creed reaches out to steady his female and turns to glare at me. "Don't be a dick."

I shift back and flip my hair forward to cover my face. "Just following your lead, asshole. Thanks for the aneurysm."

Something dark flashes in Creed's ebony gaze and I wish I could read the guy better. He's always been so guarded and miserable. Maybe the shit with me at night was all about punishment and feeling powerless.

Not that it matters now.

He's got two new shiny playthings to get him off.

The bear comes jogging out of the building. "It's a swanky, private condominium. Thirty floors with eight units per floor. If you give me the name of your witch, I'll look her up on the directory list."

Creed frowns. "I was bound to a table being poisoned. We didn't exchange contact information."

Doc holds up his palms. "Don't kill the messenger. I was trying to help."

Creed curses and rolls those big, muscled shoulders of his. "My apologies. Everything about my curse brings out the worst in me."

The guy nods. "Good thing I was raised in a sleuth of angry hotheads. Being snapped at feels like home."

And just like that, Creed's demeanor changes. The dark storm cloud that has hung over his head for as long as I've known him parts and he offers the bear a smile. "Lucky for me because I've been nothing but an angry hothead for the past two years."

"Match made in heaven."

Keyla rolls her eyes and chuckles. "What is the security like inside? Is there a concierge or a security officer we could ask about who just went inside?"

"No. It looks to be a fully-automated building."

Keyla arches her manicured brows and makes a face. "That'll be handy when AI revolts and takes over the world."

Creed rolls his eyes but it's a sweet, teasing gesture. "You're ridiculous."

Is it wrong to want to throat-punch the prince?

Asking for a friend.

"Can we get back to the slecking point? We don't know if the witch lives here or is visiting someone. We don't have any way of getting inside. And we *do* know Laryssa will kill me and likely have Honor brutalized if she finds out you're moving on the witch."

Cue four sets of piercing, icy glares.

Too bad.

My security tablet vibrates in the thigh pocket of my fatigues and I pull it out. "Slecking hell."

"What?" Creed asks.

"It's Vik. He's back from escorting the queen to the castle

and wondering where we are. There's no way we can get back to Dornte before he finds out we're in Clarinta. I'm dead."

Kotah shakes his head. "Not necessarily. If our cover story was that I wanted to make inroads with the Clarinta delegates to establish the bridging of the portal gate, let's get there and get started. Then you invite Vik to join us and he'll verify our story."

I check the time and curse. "We'd have to get back to the station hub really fast."

"We can't go now," Creed snaps. "I need to find the witch and break this fucking curse."

Keyla lays a hand on his arm and offers him a soothing smile. "There's nothing we can do on the witch front at this moment. There are two hundred and forty private residences in there and she could be in any one of them. Knowing she's here is a start. As soon as Lukas and Hawk arrive, we'll get them started on sussing out more. They are amazing at finding the hidden threads to pull on to unravel plots against us."

"Why would they help me? They don't know me."

I don't have time for Creed to get on board. With my datapad already in hand, I call up the shuttle app and order a conveyance.

A moment later one glides to a stop in front of us.

"Everyone in. We need to get back to the hub and invite the Clarinta liaison to meet us there." Creed doesn't budge and I'm about to have the second aneurysm of the hour. "Seriously, Creed. I need this. I've always tried to do right by you within the constraints of my position. Don't screw me on this."

Kotah gestures for Keyla and Doc to get in the car and sets a hand on Creed's shoulder. "I understand your hesitation to walk away from this. It's your first glimpse of hope to undo what was done to you, but you know Rhy's right. If this blood witch is as powerful as she seems, we need to formulate a solid plan and come back at this with strategic intent."

The Wolf King has some kind of magical touch because as impossible as it is, the tension in Creed's body eases and he relents.

I rush around the front hood and get in the driver's seat. Tapping the navigation panel, I key in my payment details. "Take us to the portal hub."

"Estimated time of travel is six minutes," the automated voice system says.

It will be the longest six minutes of my life.

"Contact Clarinta palace liaison, Paige Aristand, and patch through to the dash phone." I pick up the handset and hand it to the passenger seat. "You arrange your portal gate meeting and I'll respond to Vik."

And if the luck of the universe is with me, this won't blow up in my face.

CHAPTER THREE

Keyla

The car ride back to the Clarinta portal hub is almost as tense as the one with the queen this morning but thankfully not as bad as the one from the park to the castle yesterday when I was losing my mind. Huh, now that I think about it, I haven't had much luck with car rides in the Fae Realm.

Squeezing Creed's hand, I try to let him know he's not in this alone. "We'll find her. We'll track her down and figure out a way to rid you of the beast and not place Honor or anyone else in the crosshairs."

His jaw is locked so tight, I'm pretty sure he'll need dental work after this is over.

"Is there anything I can do to make you feel better?"

He lets out a long breath and lifts our joined hands to his lips. "Having you here helps. I'm fine."

No. He's not, but there's not much to be done about that right now.

Kotah finishes speaking with someone on the car phone and

hangs up the handset. "Ms. Aristand is headed to the Serenity Garden meeting room. She says she will portal there directly."

"That's good news," Rhylan says as the car pulls to the curb. "Now let's get there before Vik does."

The five of us abandon our rental car at the end of the portal station walkway and hustle our butts back inside. Rhylan leads the way through the line of glass doors, veers to the left, and rushes up a set of stairs.

We all do our best to get there quickly without flat out running and drawing attention to ourselves.

A willowy faery with pink butterfly wings pushes the door of one of the meeting rooms open and bows her head. "Prince Thornebane, it's an honor."

Creed straightens, projecting an air of calm I know he doesn't feel. "Thank you. I'd like you to meet King Nakotah Northwood of the Human Realm."

She extends her bowed head to my brother. "It's a pleasure to meet you, Majesty. I am Paige Aristand. Welcome to Clarinta."

As Creed and my brother head inside the meeting room with her, I notice five friendly—and one not so friendly—faces exiting another corridor. I point down to the main atrium and Doc grins. Pushing his fingers under his tongue, he lets off an ear-piercing whistle.

Many heads turn, but most importantly, the sound captures the attention of my brother's mates and Lukas.

The six of them jog up the steps and I welcome each with a hug... well, except Lukas—he's not much of a hugger—and Vikarus—I think he'd rather stab me than hug me.

"Welcome to the Fae Realm," I say as if I have any idea what that means.

Calli smiles and tilts her head toward Creed and Doc. "Big couple of days in the life of you, eh girlfriend?"

I hug her again. "You know it. There are so many things I

need to talk to you about. I'm glad you're here. Thank you all for coming."

"There's nowhere else we'd be, sweetheart," Jaxx says, winking at me. "Now, where is your brother?"

I gesture to the meeting room behind us. "He's in there with the Clarinta liaison talking about establishing the portal bridge."

"That's our cue." Hawk gestures to Lukas and then the two of them continue inside to join the discussions in the meeting room.

I open my mouth to let them know we need their help on the blood witch matter but with Vikarus staring at us, now is not the time.

"Boys," Brant says, addressing the twins. "If one of these other rooms is available, could we get out of the corridor and sit down? We've got a baby on board and our phoenix needs her rest and to stay off her feet."

"Good call, Bear," Jaxx says. "And what about food? Any chance this terminal has a food court?"

Calli rolls her eyes and chuckles. "Save me from well-meaning mates."

Vikarus makes no attempt to answer, but Rhylan presses his datapad over the electronic screen beside the door of the next room and opens it for us. "Feel free to take a seat."

I take him up on that, grab Calli's arm, and tug her inside with me. "Thank you, Rhylan."

The look he gives me in return isn't so much hostile as it is filled with an Arctic chill.

We get inside the meeting room and Calli's green eyes widen. "What's that about?"

I wait to see if we're going to be inundated by mates but Doc and Brant seem to have taken up guarding the door and Jaxx and Rhylan have gone down the stairs in search of food.

"Oh, I have so much to tell you but are you okay with keeping it just between us? Creed and Doc are both proud and volatile right now and I wouldn't want things discussed among the group."

Calli crosses her heart. "As long as you're not in danger and they don't need to know, then they won't hear it from me."

I point to the chairs at the end of the conference room table and we sit. "Okay, where to begin. First off..." I tell Calli about mating Creed on the mental plane and him inviting Doc into our mating and how even though it's what I wanted, Doc doesn't seem too happy about it yet.

"It's very new and male pride is real. The balance, in the beginning, is tough. When we started, there was a lot of friction between Hawk and the others. It took some work, but I broke through the barriers he had erected and showed the others the other side of him."

I sigh. "I think their tension is less about each other and more about me."

"Then it's your job to reassure them both. Maybe that's about one-on-one time or maybe it's about the three of you as a couple."

"That's another thing I need your advice on."

"What's that?"

I hesitate to even mention it, but I need insight. I don't usually feel as young and inexperienced as the number on my license indicates, but regarding how to juggle this many men, I'm out of my depths.

"This has to stay in the vault. It's personal and dangerous for me to talk about."

Calli's expression tightens. "Absolutely. You have my word."

I lean in close and lower my voice. "I think there's something between Creed and Rhylan."

"I'm not surprised. I got that vibe back in the clearing but at the time I thought the dragons were his bodyguards, not his prison guards."

"The first night we snuggled together to sleep, I smelled

Rhylan on his skin. I asked him about it later and he freaked out. After he calmed down and realized I was worried about him and not being nosy, he admitted there have been moments of the two of them together."

"And you're wondering what?"

"I'm wondering if I should bring up Rhylan joining us. Creed invited Doc into our mating bed for me. I wondered about doing the same for him."

Calli considers that for a moment and then shakes her head. "My advice is to wait. Sure, the two of them might've worked off some hostility physically but that doesn't mean he's a good fit for your marriage. You need time to assess him as a person and make sure you can trust him as part of your group."

"I get that. Yeah, I suppose I'm in a bit of a mating mood after watching your quint develop."

She smiles. "The difference is, we were tied by the prophecy from the beginning. The mating bound all five of us at once. Rhylan is currently fighting for the wrong team. He's on Laryssa's payroll and until that changes, he's more of a liability than an asset."

I hear the warning in her words and despite wanting to argue on his behalf, she's right. Maybe what Creed and Rhylan had was just working off pent-up energy.

In which case, he wouldn't be a good fit.

"Okay, thanks. That makes sense. I'll slow things down and wait on the R-factor."

"I think that's best."

There's a knock on the door and then Jaxx, Brant, and Doc shuffle into the room carrying trays of food.

"Lunch is served, ladies. There's a big ol' city beneath this place," Jaxx says.

"Well, we won't go hungry anytime soon, that's for sure." Calli laughs as the guys set the trays down. "Do we know what this is?"

Jaxx winks. "Not really, but it smelled good and the dragon pointed out the things to avoid. He may be a bit standoffish, but I think he's comin' around to us a bit."

I hope so. I honestly do.

Glancing over Brant's shoulder, I'm glad to see the door is shut. "Okay, before we're interrupted, Doc and I need to fill you in on why we really came to this realm. If we can't get time alone with Hawk and Lukas, tell them we need help finding the blood witch who cursed Creed."

Creed

Sitting next to Hawk's bodyguard and right-hand man in the meeting I wonder if he's as good as Keyla and Doc believe him to be. The outcome of my entire future depends on him finding that witch and helping us figure out how to break her curse.

It guts me that I left that building without answers.

I understand the logic that I couldn't stand on the sidewalk indefinitely and then strangle her when she emerged, but it felt like another round of brutal torture to walk away.

"I see no issue with that," the Clarinta liaison says.

"Wonderful." Kotah offers Ms. Aristand a warm smile and then looks toward Hawk to see if he has anything to add to the conversation.

The way Kotah and Hawk interact is impressive. For only knowing one another a few months and being forced into a mating like Keyla and I are, they appear to be genuinely happy and at ease with one another.

I realize trust is earned, but there also has to be a willingness to allow someone to earn it.

I check myself inwardly and chuckle. When did I become such a damned sap? A week ago I hated everyone and wanted to slit throats and make Vik and Rhy clean up the entrails. Funny how life spins out of control when you're not looking.

I wonder what Keyla's doing right now.

She's likely tucked herself into a corner girl-talking with the phoenix. From what I gather and what I saw in the clearing when we arrived, Calli and Keyla are close.

Which sucks for me because I certainly didn't make a stellar first impression on any of them.

"I think that's all we need," Hawk says, breaking me out of my thoughts. The avian is the lead alpha of their quint. He's tall and chiseled and with the expensive clothes and the tattoos, he's something to look at. "Do you have anything else you'd like to discuss, my King?"

Something lights in Kotah's eyes as Hawk calls him that. No one introduced him as Kotah's mate, so I didn't bring it up. It seems Hawk calling him that is some kind of inside joke.

"I think that's everything," Kotah says rising from his chair. "Once we visit Rames and Travon we'll have all the coordinates and be able to finalize the portal bridges. We look forward to hosting delegates from your quadrant in the Human Realm while you explore life on the other side of the rift."

"It's an exciting time indeed," Paige says, her pink wings fluttering gently behind her. Once she zips her portfolio closed, she presses her fist to her right shoulder and bows, as is the custom. "Peace and happiness."

"And also to you," Kotah says.

When the faery leaves, Lukas stands and heads toward the door.

I raise my hand. "One moment. May I speak with you before you leave, Lukas… and you, as well Hawk, if that's all right?"

Hawk's gaze narrows but when Kotah nods, he seems to relax a little. "Okay, let me check that the girls are taken care of, and then I'm all yours."

"I'll go," Kotah says. "This is important and I haven't seen Calli yet."

"She missed you boys last night, Wolf," Hawk says, grinning at his mate. "Yeah, go say hi."

It's funny, as Kotah steps away and I realize how badly I need their help, my stomach kicks up a fuss.

"Are you well, Creed?" Kotah says, turning back to grip my arm. The connection of skin-on-skin brings a wave of soothing warmth and my nerves settle.

"What is it you do when you're near people?"

He releases my arm and blushes. "Apologies. I forget sometimes…."

"No, it's fine, I just… I've been angry for so long, it's a little unnerving when you're near me and it eases and then, right now when you touched me, it's like a balm to the anguish that burns inside me."

"Kotah is an omega," Hawk says, his gaze sharp as he assesses me. "It's a natural affinity. We call him a bullshit buffer but it goes beyond that. His compassion knows no bounds and he is hands down the smartest, most genuine person you will ever have the honor of meeting."

Kotah looks up at the ceiling and chuckles. "Laying it on a little thick, aren't you? Are you plying me with compliments in the hopes you'll get lucky later?"

Hawk grins. "Is it working?"

"Was there any doubt?"

Keyla comes through the closed door and chuckles. "You'll have to excuse my brother and his mates. They make no secret about their physical attraction to one another. You'll get used to it."

Hawk winks. "Hey, Princess. How is mated life treating you?"

She hugs him and then comes to my side to slide her arm around my waist. "So far so good. But honestly, I'm ready to get back to the castle and spend some alone time. Things have been so rushed I feel like I'm falling downhill and can't quite get my footing."

"I know that feeling," Hawk says. "Is Calli good?"

Keyla laughs. "Brant and Jaxx brought up half the food court and are feeding your young."

Hawk and Kotah both grin and seem to relax. Hawk brings his attention back to me. "Alrighty then. What is it you wanted to discuss?"

I check that the door is still closed and draw a steadying breath. "I realize you don't know me and I was a royal pain in the ass when we arrived even when you tried to extend a welcome, but I need a favor. Keyla suggested that the two of you are the men to talk to."

She seems to gauge my discomfort and takes over. "Since the moment our searing took hold, we've been pulled by an unrelenting force toward something. At first, it was what drove us to run for the rift after our searing, now we're certain it's destiny's design for us and has something to do with Creed breaking Laryssa's curse on him and reclaiming his throne."

Hawk nods. "Okay, I'm with you so far. We pieced together as much ourselves."

"Well, a few hours ago, that calling pulled us into the path of the blood witch who cursed him with the demon wolf. We followed her through the Clarinta hub and to a building not far from here. We don't have a name but we all got a good look at her and are hoping she lives in the building."

"So you need us to find out who she is and assess what we're up against," Hawk says.

I nod. "I haven't given you any reason to want to help me but—"

Hawk raises a hand. "Save it. You're Keyla's mate. She's our little sister. As long as you're good to her and honor your mating, you are family. If you color outside the lines, all bets are off and—royalty or not—I *will* bury you where no one will find the body."

"*Noice,*" Calli says, coming in to join the party. "It's been hours since we threatened to murder and bury people. Now it's a party."

"Did someone say party?" Jaxx says, leaning into the room. "I'm game."

Keyla laughs. "You are always game for a party."

"That is true, sweetheart. So, where and when?"

"Back to the castle, right now?" Vikarus says. "Your portal gate business is done for the day. We need to get Prince Creed back."

Jaxx grins. "Party at your place it is. Do you have supplies or should we stop on the way home?"

I blink at Keyla, not sure how to take any of this.

"Like I said. You'll get used to them."

CHAPTER FOUR

Doc

By the time we get back to the Thornebane Castle, it's mid-afternoon and everyone decides to retreat to their corners for a few hours before dinner and what we're calling a 'Drink and Think'. Party seemed inappropriate considering Creed's current situation.

Which, who are we kidding, is Jaxx's way to have a party even with so much pressing down on us.

I'm okay with that. I could use a drink.

Keyla, Creed, and I arrive back at the royal suite and that's when it dawns on us that things are awkward. I want Keyla naked. By the arousal I've smelled coming off Creed more than once today, he wants Keyla naked. And Keyla has been more than open about the fact that she wants us naked.

"Okay, not to be weird or indelicate here, but how the hell are we doing this?" I ask. "It's crude to ask, but are we taking turns or what?"

Keyla frowns. "It's not crude. You're curious and want to communicate. That's fine."

"I say we start with drinking," Creed says. "Perhaps a lot of drinking."

Keyla's frown grows. "Is the idea of us being together really that uncomfortable for the two of you?"

Creed meets my gaze and the two of us nod at the same time.

"Yeah, babe. It's a little uncomfortable. I think drinking is the way to go."

I hate the tightening of her smile but there's no sense lying to her. "It's different for you, Princess. You know me and love me. You're bound to him and feel the pull of building something solid with him. Creed and I have neither of those things."

"What we do have," Creed says, joining in, "is our shared affection for you and our commitment to make this work."

Keyla toes off her shoes and drops them by the door. "All right, then I suggest we take a page out of Jaxx's book. Instead of drinking for the sake of getting drunk, let's play a drinking game geared to get to know one another better."

I laugh and meet Creed's ebony gaze. "Fair warning, all Jaxx's drinking games end up with people naked and having sex."

Creed's silver brow arches. "Consider me warned. Since that is the desired end-game, we'll proceed."

Prince Thornebane returns to the door, turns the latch, and the heavy *clack* of the deadbolt signals we are free to begin.

I head straight for the bar and start flipping tumblers up. "Keyla prefers mixed fruity drinks but it looks like the selections are whiskey, a stout ale, and something dark burgundy."

"That's haze," Creed says. "It's tasty and fruity but its name is apt. It sneaks up on you and leaves you in a haze."

I uncork the top and it smells a little like red licorice. "Done. I think a haze is the way to go."

"Pour me one, too," Creed says. "And since we're here for the night, you might as well use full-sized glasses. It'll save trips to the bar."

"A man of strategic planning." I exchange the tumblers for taller glasses and pour two. "What about you, Princess?"

"Whiskey neat."

I hear the tension in her voice and check on her. "Everything okay?"

She lifts a shoulder but it's obviously not. "I think I owe you both an apology. I wanted this because it's what I wanted, but I'm realizing now how selfish that was. I watched Kotah's life bloom with his mates and maybe I got carried away with the idea that we could have it all."

I hate the sad, self-recrimination in her tone and walk the drinks over. Keyla accepts hers and sits on the edge of a long, over-stuffed four-seater sofa by the fireplace, Creed sits beside her and leans back against the cushions, and I sit on the marble-topped coffee table opposite them.

"Is this trio what I pictured the past three months? No. Is there a small part of me still mourning the life I envisioned for us? Yes. But don't think for a moment I regret where we are. *You* are my mate. *You* are my home. And yes, I agree. I've seen the quint grow from behind closed doors like you have and think it's fucking awesome. But it didn't happen on day one or even on day three and that's where we are."

Creed sits up and strokes a gentle hand over her knee. "I'll warm up to things, I promise. A week ago, I had no one in my corner and no one I could trust. Now, I've got you and Dillan, and I seem to have inherited an entourage of family supporters. We're not against any of it. We're just saying—and correct me if I'm wrong, and speaking out of turn, Bear—that taking a beat to breathe without expectations would be welcome."

I nod. "Yeah, taking a beat would be nice."

I watch Keyla's expression as that sinks in. "All right, that's fair."

Except I smell her disappointment.

It's not very often her youthful inexperience comes into play, but I think that's all this is. I'm her first real boyfriend and that compounded into a three-way marriage. Even though she wanted it first and most, I think she needs to slow down a bit too.

"All right." I set my glass on the floor next to the couch they're on and then move the floral centerpiece to the floor as well. "Help me move this coffee table."

Creed hands Keyla his glass and moves to take the other end. Yes, I'm a bear and yes, I could do it myself, but it's his furniture and a little teamwork can't hurt.

"Fuck, this thing weighs a ton."

Creed chuckles. "It's made out of a sheet of solid stone."

"Good point." We get the stone slab shifted to behind the couch and that leaves us with two massive couches facing one another and what is probably a million-dollar rug in between. I undo the button of my jeans and settle on the floor with my back to the couch opposite Keyla.

When I'm settled, I reclaim my drink. "Okay, the game is two truths and a lie. Each time one of us guesses someone's lie, we get one action. This means, I might want a kiss from Keyla or she might want me to take off my shirt. We'll start with easy actions at first, so nothing too demanding. One win, one action. If no one guesses the lie, the two guessing have to drink."

Keyla beams. "Got it."

Creed frowns. "But can't wildlings scent lies in the air? How is that fair?"

"It's true, we can." I pull a purple flower out of the arrangement and hand it to Keyla, and then choose a blue one for myself. "That's why Keyla and I will have to fill our sense of smell with something else."

Keyla's face falls. "Oh, I thought you were rigging it so we could win."

I laugh. "No. If you win all the time, Creed and I will end up naked and making out and we're not there yet. We want a chance to get you, too. Don't we, mate?"

Creed nods. "Definitely."

"Okay, I'll start." I hold up my glass and point for Keyla to sniff her flower. "I had a brief stint as a stripper in Las Vegas. I once robbed a bank. I'm squeamish about needles."

Keyla bursts out laughing and sits deeper into the couch, tucking her feet under her. "Well, you're a field medic and doctor, so I don't think it's needles. I'm going with stripper being the lie."

Creed laughs. "Since I know nothing about you, I'll go with Keyla's doctor theory and pick bank robbery. You don't seem like the type to me."

I grin. "Keyla drinks. I was at a bachelor party weekend in Vegas a couple of years ago. I got really drunk and joined the Thunder From Down Under from the audience. The next night, they asked me back for an encore up on stage."

Keyla's belly laugh is the sweetest sound ever.

"So, am I right?" Creed asks.

I shake my head. "You're drinking too, my friend. One of my first ex-military jobs was for a security company that pokes holes in systems considered to be impenetrable. I absolutely robbed a bank."

Creed lifts his glass and takes a long drink.

"Okay, who's next?"

Rhylan

The thick, rubber soles of my boots beat off a steady rhythm as Vik and I respond to the summons from on high. I knew it would come, yet still, I'm not looking forward to it.

The first time Vik and I came into the throne room of the

Dornte quadrant we were twelve years old. Our father, Shadrick Silverwing was the second in command of the wildling dragons and we were on the fast track to a life of success and respect.

Born into one of the oldest families in the strongest wildling species, we were young princes in our own rite.

Then our brood Alpha, Shadowcaster set his sights on our mother and our lives turned to shit.

So, yeah, maybe I sympathize with Creed and what he's been put through. Maybe I'm jealous. Not about the female—no, I couldn't give a shit about her—but about the fact that the universe swooped in and offered him a chance to set it right.

Where's my chance?

The guard outside the throne room opens the eight-foot panel of wood and allows us entrance. "She has been waiting."

I'm sure she has.

Heads held high, Vik and I enter, shoulder to shoulder. Despite what the world sees, we're not bookends. Yes, we're identical in appearance, but we're not the same person. Vik is a good soldier—a great soldier—but he lacks foresight and doesn't think past his orders.

He also doesn't wonder if we're on the right side.

Honestly, I don't think he cares. He's here because we're duty-bound and that's the end of it.

The queen is listening to one of her rich and shady supporters complain about something, so Vik and I step off to the side and stand at attention to wait our turn.

When the man has had his say, he waits for Laryssa's response. Whatever he's hoping for doesn't materialize because, after a moment, he gives up, drops his chin, and backs away.

Most people know better than to turn their back on Queen Laryssa.

We know better than to advance.

When she's ready, she turns her head and points to the floor in front of her. Both of us move in to take a knee at her feet.

Again my memory flips back to the time we visited with our father. Creed's father, King Thornebane sat on that same throne and practically sucked the air out of the room. He was an impressive and intimidating man and what's more... he never forced anyone to take a knee.

If you chose to bow to him, that was your call but he never demanded it.

He didn't need the boost to his ego.

Laryssa falls short of him on all fronts. "Tell me about your day, Rhylan, and make it good."

The acerbic tone doesn't bode well and I draw a deep breath. "The day didn't go as planned, Majesty. The Wolf King opted to go to Clarinta to further his mission to establish the portal bridges with the other quadrants."

"I permitted you to accompany them on a tour of Dornte starting at the archive exhibits. I did not approve you leaving the quadrant with Creed and strengthening the Wolf King's foothold in this realm."

"I apologize. Sincerely. I put my foot down and objected. It fell on deaf ears. Short of shifting and physically air-lifting Creed and Nakotah back here, there was nothing I could do to keep them from crossing into Clarinta."

"Creed has become emboldened with his mating," Vikarus adds. "He's found an ally in his brother-in-law and is becoming a problem."

Slecking hell.

My head turns on a pivot and I glare at my twin. He likely thinks he's helping me by throwing Creed and the Wolf King in the fire, but dangling their insolence in front of Laryssa serves no one.

"Yes. I've noticed. Do you know how I noticed?"

I can tell by the tone of her lead in that I'm not going to like what comes next. Still, I have no choice but to respond. "How is that, my queen?"

Laryssa picks up the datapad from the table beside her throne and calls up a video. "It seems Creed and the Wolf King seized an impromptu press opportunity to bring the citizens the good news about the opening of the portal to the Human Realm. A portal *I* worked tirelessly to secure for months."

Yeah, except your plans with the Black Knight dissident fell through and your military coup d'etat never got off the ground.

"Explain to me how this happened, Rhylan?"

"The prince kissed his bride inside the hub and by the time they parted, there was a swarm of curious citizens closing in. He announced Keyla and Dillan as his mates and then explained who they were and how they came together. I don't believe there was any intention of undermining your role in establishing the first contact."

The queen doesn't seem pleased, but she also doesn't argue. "And they are secured in the suite now?"

Vik nods. "Yes, Majesty. Creed and his two mates and the Wolf King and his four mates."

She blinks. "The phoenix and all the guardians are here?"

I nod. "They arrived while the Wolf King was speaking to the Clarinta liaison about establishing their bridge."

Laryssa frowns. "Clarinta having access to the Human Realm wasn't part of my plans. I need to know if I can salvage any of my original objectives. Vikarus, you will go to StoneHaven and speak with the travelers. I want Sebastian Whitehouse's other son tracked down. What was his name?"

"Hunter," Vik says.

"Yes. Find him. We didn't work so hard to put this pup king into power just to have him find his spine and steal my rule. I was assured once the boy's father was dead, the realm would fall to me."

Except the fae universe stepped in and gave Kotah the backup he needs to rise to the occasion.

It makes me wonder about Creed's searing. As much as it bugs me to be his enemy, now I feel like I'm the enemy of the cosmic plan as well.

If Kotah's mating was to get him ready to lead the Human Realm then it makes sense that Creed and Keyla's mating is to give him the strength he needs to reclaim his power.

"Rhylan? Is there a problem?"

I blink and realize Vik has stopped halfway to the exit and turned back wondering why I'm not leaving.

Oh, we've been dismissed.

"Apologies, my queen. No problem. I simply got lost in my thoughts. Peace and blessings." Dipping my chin, I back away and stride across the throne room floor to catch up with Vik.

"You okay?" he asks as we exit.

"Yeah, fine. Just a lot on my mind. Before you do anything, let me know what you find out about Hunter and the queen's plans."

He snorts. "Don't you think the queen should be the first to hear that info?"

I shake my head. "No. I don't. The tides of power are shifting, Vik. We've got to be very careful of our footing or the ground will crumble beneath us. Promise me you'll bring it to me first."

Vik shrugs looking bored. "Sure. I'll let you know."

Good. That's good. I have a feeling how we handle things from here on out will determine our future. "All right. I'll head back to the suite and keep an eye on Creed and his company. You be careful."

CHAPTER FIVE

Keyla

*A*pparently, without my sense of smell, I am a terrible lie detector. I've lost my pants, shirt, bra, and panties and am on my fourth drink. Creed and Dillan are still way too covered up. "I feel silly wearing only socks."

Doc chuckles. "I don't know. I like the look. What do you think, mate?"

Creed laughs. "I like the socks. I like it more if they were leather boots or heels, too."

Doc whistles and nods his head. "Definitely leather boots. Let's make that happen."

I let them have their moment without protest. Maybe common goals will help them find common ground. "All right, I offer you carte blanche. If you guys buy it, I'll wear it. How's that?"

Doc's brow arches. "Hells, yes. Challenge accepted. I'm sure, between the two of us, we can come up with a few ideas."

Creed chuckles. "I know our little wolf has a few ideas of her own. Has she mentioned to you she fantasizes about men in leather bondage shorts?"

The look on Doc's face is too funny. I wave away the look he gives me. "All right. Whose turn is it?"

"Mine," Creed says. "You both guessed wrong, so I get two actions."

I point at my socks. "Let me guess."

"Hardly. I'm not wasting my time on your socks. My first action is that the bear takes his boxers off."

Doc pegs him with a look, downs his drink, and stands up to oblige. With sure action, he shoves the cotton underwear down his muscled thighs and steps free of them. Widening his stance a little, he adjusts the lay of things now getting aired out.

"And your second request?" Doc asks.

"Keyla should go down on you and suck you off."

My wolf lets off a growl. "Yes, please."

"I don't know what you've done and not done before, Little Wolf, but if there's ever something you're not fond of, you need to be honest about it."

"Oh, I'm happy to suck on him but it was your wish. Are you sure you don't want me to suck on you?"

Creed is leaning back on the sofa, his boxers firmly filled out at the front with an arousal to be proud of. "Don't worry about me. Watching you get your bear off is a give and take. You give him pleasure and I take pleasure from it in return."

Doc is already sitting on the rug so I point for him to lie down. "Do you mind?" I know he doesn't.

He's bare from the waist down and sporting one heck of an ode to getting sexy. Not to mention the scent of his hunger filling the air. "Who am I to argue with our host?"

Creed tosses a cushion to where my bear is stretched out like an offering ready to be devoured. It hits him in the face and my prince chuckles. "Nice catch."

Doc reaches back and places the cushion behind his neck.

The movement stretches out his torso and gives me all kinds of inspiration.

Coming in from the side, I crawl into position and grip his shaft. The contact has his cock jumping in my hand and his bear lets off a deep, raspy grumble.

I give him a moment to settle.

Even though oral is something we've explored, it adds a new dimension to have Creed there watching.

"Would you like to walk me through what you want or shall I take it from here?" I glance up and Creed is taking off his pants and tossing them on the floor beside the couch.

He lowers his chin and looks at me through hooded eyes. "Oh, I'm calling the play-by-play. I take it you two have played this game before?"

"It's one of my favorites," I say.

"All right, then let's not keep you from something you love. Give him a few strokes and greet him properly."

The strength and command in his voice are laced with seduction. It pushes at me with an almost tangible force and I realize he's unleashing his gift on us. Not that I mind. When he used it during sex when it was just the two of us, it surrounded me and brought me to another level of pleasure.

It was incredible.

My eyes close as I'm bombarded by a surge of arousal. I bite my lip and focus on the task at hand. Doc's cock is solid steel beneath a silk sheath. I tighten my grip as I slide my hold root to tip and back again.

"Good girl. Now lean in and suck on the swollen crown. Draw your tongue around the tip of his cock."

I follow his instructions and savor the scent that I've grown so accustomed to.

My bear's arousal is natural and woodsy. It's possessive. It's addictive.

"Now swirl your tongue around the rim. Trace that

engorged head and then lift up and slip the tip of your tongue into the opening."

I do as I'm told and Doc lets off a hiss.

"See how much your boy likes that," Creed says. "Did he spill for you just then, Little Wolf?"

He did.

My wolf howls within as the scent of his cum hits my senses. I gather the pearl of salty cream from his tip and swallow. "Mhmmm."

"Doc, now it's your turn. You're a strong boy. Grab our girl by the hips and swing her over your head so you can tongue her in return."

My legs are swung around so I'm kneeling over his shoulders and he's sixty-nineing me. My heart's raging beat pounds inside my chest.

Yes. I want this. Bad.

Having them both here spurs on a wild desire in me.

"Test the waters and tell me, Bear. Is she wet?"

The scruff of Doc's jaw rubs the inside of my legs. I sigh as his tongue sweeps the length of my folds and flicks the opening of my pussy in long, leisurely strokes. "A good start, but she can do much better. Our girl gets so wet you can lap at her like a thirsty predator."

Creed chuckles. "Did you hear that, Keyla? Our bear says you can do better. He's thirsty and you've got more in you to give. Bear, I want you to dig in and make her legs quiver. Take your time. The longer it takes building her up, the better it'll be."

A low rumble vibrates against my core and the primitive sound sends goosebumps racing across my skin. I brace one arm against the carpet and grind back against Doc's mouth.

"That's it," Creed rasps. "Ride his mouth and at the same time, keep tonguing that slit of his. Press the tip of your tongue in and flick around. Don't worry about it hurting him. I guarantee you that sting feels amazing. Doesn't it, Bear?"

"Fuck, yeah," he breathes arching his hips. I stroke up and down the length of his shaft with my mouth a few times.

"Keyla, when you bob your head up and down, let your teeth gently score his shaft. Then, when he starts pumping his hips, ease back and tongue the slit again. Go ahead, and have some fun. I'm going to sit back and stroke off to the view for a bit. Bear, how's she tasting?"

"So, fucking good." He nuzzles rougher, nipping at my clit and sucking the tender nub of nerves with his teeth. A rush of moisture meets his mouth and my nipples harden even tighter. "That's my girl. Now we're getting somewhere."

I groan as he grips my hips and forces my thighs wider so he has more room to move. Doc is a black bear, so even though he doesn't have the massive size of Brant as a grizzly, he's still a stocky, well-built male.

"Bear, our girl's a greedy little minx. Fuck her with your fingers."

I groan as he obeys.

Before now, Doc has always been so careful when fingering me, determined not to break the seal of my virginity. That's over now.

Creed's calling his bear forward.

When Doc's fingers impale me I push back and revel in the greedy clench and pull of my inner muscles around those digits. He is a welcome presence in my body, stretching me... teasing, and touching me.

The steady *click, click, click* of Creed palming a damp cock is too good not to lift my head. Gripping Doc at the root of his erection, I raise my gaze and growl.

Creed is manspreading on the couch above us, pumping a hand up and down with a violent rhythm. His shirt is unbuttoned and hanging open to expose all that toned musculature.

I soak in the sights, my gaze drawn to the beauty of his lineage tattoo down his side.

One day, I will learn to read what it says.

He catches me staring, his attention searingly intense. With our gazes locked a wave of need zings straight to my core. "Do you like what you see, Little Wolf?"

"Yes."

"Bear, do you have any hangups I should know about?"

"None. I'm good."

"Then wet your thumb and play at the rim of her ass. Don't impale her yet, just play. Our minxy mate likes a little rough and dirty, don't you?"

"Yes." I make a small, helpless sound as that thumb comes into play. Doc refused to engage this side of me. I don't know if he didn't believe me or didn't want to believe me, but this is too good to pretend I don't love it.

It's teasing torture, pressing against sensitive nerve endings. Calling something wild in me. Desperate, I brace my palms against the carpet and suck on him with everything I've got.

"Feel the pleasure ripple through you, angel. Is your arousal brewing like a storm inside you?"

I nod.

"Then tell Doc if you want more. Do you want that thumb to do more than tease?"

I nod.

"Give her more, Bear."

I cry out as the teasing becomes an intense burn and then a fierce pleasure. Whatever reservations Doc had before, seem to be gone.

"Take from him, Keyla. Ride his mouth and push back. More, Bear. Claim her inside and out."

I can't breathe. I arch my back and climax in a shattering blast. My release robs me of sight and scent of breath and heartbeat.

The pleasure is deep, endless. Consuming.

Doc

As Keyla comes apart, my bear lets off a long, lusty growl. The two of us have shared plenty of playful orgasms but nothing like this. Keyla's wolf is close to the surface and taking everything I give her with greedy, hungry pulls.

She told me all along not to treat her like a princess and I never realized how much of a disservice it's been to both of us.

As she pushes back on my thumb and comes against my mouth, she's as wild as I've ever seen her.

"Are you ready to be fucked, Little Wolf?" Creed's voice is rough and deep.

"Yes," she pants. "Hard and wild, like before."

"That's my girl."

Only, she's *my* girl. Or at least I thought she was.

Maybe part of my issue with sharing her is thinking that she and I had things locked down perfectly. The silver-haired prince is showing me up.

"Swing around and kiss your bear while I fill you."

It surprises me that Keyla complies without hesitation. She trusts him to pleasure her and damn, as much as that's a hit to my ego, it's also sexy as hell.

Keyla climbs up my side, the warm mounds of her breasts dancing in a glorious, weighted dangle and sway. When she reaches my shoulders, she lowers her lips to mine and reaches down my chest to grasp my cock. "Hello, Bear. Are you good?"

Am I? I see the apprehensive light flickering in her eyes and a shiver runs through me. She's still worried about my reaction. I committed to this when I accepted Creed's offer to join the mating. As Kotah so eloquently put it, I committed to twice the mating fun, not half.

"Yeah, I'm great. Kiss me."

She leans in and her mouth slides over mine and at the same time, her grip tightens and she starts stroking.

"You look good on all fours," Creed says, positioning behind her.

Yeah, Keyla on all fours is a sight to see whether in wolf form or like this. She's too busy kissing the hell outta me to respond. Her tongue breaks the seal of my mouth and she invades and challenges me.

Before Creed, she never asserted herself like this. I was the dominant one. Now, it seems, she's found her inner vixen.

When she slows our kiss and breaks off with a gasp, I shift my gaze to watch Creed's face as he sinks into Keyla's heat. Damn. I've only got to experience that mind-blowing pleasure once myself.

I need inside her again.

"How good does that feel, amirite?"

Creed opens his eyes and for once, those ebony demon eyes don't freak me out. They aren't emotionless voids as I used to see. There is a great deal of communication in them if you take the time to look. "She's so tight and hungry."

I reach around her shoulders, holding her so she can sink forward and not worry about holding herself up. When she's secured I meet Creed's gaze and nod. "I've got her. Do your thing."

The uneven smirk that lifts the side of the prince's mouth is sexy as fuck. With a sweep of his hand, he gathers her hair and wraps it in his fist. Tugging back pulls her head up and I get a glorious whiff of the spike in her arousal.

"Oh, fuck, she loves that. You should smell the sweet decadence of her scent right now."

He tugs again and the burgundy choker covering her throat shifts as she swallows. "More, Little Wolf?"

"Yes, please."

"Such nice manners."

I chuckle. Nice manners, sure, but that doesn't mean she isn't digging her nails into my cock. Which I'll never complain about because fuck as much as it stings… it's so worth it.

Creed picks up speed and then he's thrusting his hips forward, again and again, pounding hard and deep. I worry about the rate he's penetrating her but I don't need to. By the scent of pleasure she's giving off, he's driving her toward another consuming orgasm.

I tighten my grip on her shoulders, holding her in place as the rhythmic slap of flesh-on-flesh drives me insane with lust.

Fuck. I want to do this to her. To key her up and hit her with everything I've got.

And, if I'm being honest, I wouldn't mind being on the receiving end of that kind of power thrusting either.

The pressure building in my balls burns to break free but I'll be damned if I'm the first to let go.

My bear lets off a long rumble as I bite back the urge to come. Keyla shows me no mercy though. She seems to remember she was palming me before the fae prince started giving her insides a rubdown and goes back to pumping my cock.

My chest heaves, my abs clenched so hard the muscles are solid stone. I can't fight the release.

With a curse and a long, guttural groan, I give in, my body flexing as I succumb.

CHAPTER SIX

Creed

The bear's mighty body flexes and quakes as he empties streams of cream across his ridged abs. The look on his face is tortured ecstasy. He's laying it all out. Stiff and panting, with his eyes clamped closed, Doc is something to see.

My thigh muscles are on fire, my abs burning. Keyla will be the death of me, I swear. Because no matter how deep I get inside her, it only makes me want her more. The slap of my tingling balls against the soft curves of her thighs is driving me mad.

I need to own her... to consume her... to possess her body and soul.

I feel her quickening take hold as her core grips my cock. With every squeeze and pulse, her body milks me. It's too much... and at the same time, not enough.

I open a mental channel between the three of us and her climax hits me hard. Fuck. I can't fight it. Thrusting forward with a ferocity I've never felt during sex before, I lock my hips and my climax takes over.

Keyla's body is constricting around me in slick, greedy pulls and the room spins.

The instant my orgasm hits, my hips spear her hard and freeze for a split second before withdrawing an inch and then driving deep for another kicking explosion.

I come so hard, my vision fails me.

Dizzy and slick with sweat, I collapse to the carpet and roll onto my back. The fight to fill my heaving lungs is real. I'm panting, my breath coming in quick, shallow bursts. Staring up at the ceiling, I let off a groan. "That was…"

"Fucking hot," Doc says. "Nicely done, mate."

When his fist raises into the air, I meet his knuckles with my own. Then, I roll onto my side and lick the soft flesh of Keyla's arm. "How are you, Little Wolf? I'm sorry if I was too rough. I used you hard but you seemed to enjoy it."

Keyla barks a laugh. "That was amazing."

"You'll be sore."

"I don't care. Like I told you. I want it all. No holds barred. Never think for me."

With the mental connection open, I feel the stab of regret those words trigger in our third. Keyla misses it, and that's good. She shouldn't feel guilty about expressing her needs.

I meet Doc's gaze and offer him a sympathetic smile as I open a private conversation. *Maybe you were a little too much of a gentleman for her tastes, but this is where we are now. Don't regret what the two of you shared. It was who you were at that time.*

Why the fuck didn't I listen when she told me she wanted more?

You saw her age, inexperience, and station and wanted to ensure you didn't overwhelm or overstep. That's not a bad thing. It shows you're a good guy.

He chuckles. *And so, what does that make you, the bad boy?*

I waggle my eyebrows. *I can live with that.*

I probe around in the emotions swirling in Dillan's mind

and am pleased to find no regrets about joining us. He's still very turned on and not only by Keyla.

My balls tingle with the awakening of a second wave on the horizon. *What's on your mind, Bear? Is there something I can do for you?*

He meets my gaze and frowns.

Sorry. Mind fae. Me reading your mental impulses is very similar to you smelling emotions. I don't mean it to be invasive, but if you're still hungry, I've got another round or two in me.

Doc leans back against the sofa, stretching out all those sculpted, wildling muscles. *What does that look like?*

Whatever you want it to look like. I'm usually the driver but if you've got something specific in mind, I'm game. I don't want you with needs that aren't met. I meant what I said about this mating. You're not only here because of Keyla. I think we can build something.

He thinks about that for a few more seconds and then nods. *Yeah, let's get the first time under our belts while things are still sexy and the haze of booze is hanging thick.*

I rise onto my elbow and trace a gentle finger up Keyla's belly and around her nipples. The gentle sawing of her breath is so cute.

She dozed off, sated and tired right out.

How about we move her onto the sofa and take it into the bedroom, so we don't disturb her?

With a nod, he scoops our mate off the carpet and gently sets her onto the sofa. I jog into Honor's room and grab one of the ultra-soft throw blankets my sister loves so much.

When Keyla is settled and covered, Dillan and I head into the bedroom. We leave the door open to make it clear she's welcome to join us if she wakes up. Otherwise, this will remain a get-to-know-you guy session.

～

Doc

Holy fuck, am I ready for this? I watch the chiseled pull and stretch of Creed's bare legs and tight ass as he leads us back to his bedroom. He's still wearing his dress shirt unbuttoned and open at the front. It's a hot look for him. Most things are a hot look for him.

The problem isn't the physical act of fucking around. I'm a bear wildling. I can do that. The guy is ripped and broody and I'm a sucker for an emotionally tortured soul.

My hesitation falls squarely in the 'am I ready to accept everything this implies'?

"Give me two minutes," Creed says, stepping into the ensuite bathroom.

I stare at the bed and think about the past twenty-four hours: Keyla and Creed collapsing together after almost dying, Creed inviting me to join them, him and Keyla having mind sex, then her and I finally mating...

A lot has happened but when I do a gut check and ask my bear what he thinks, he's a solid yes.

Make this work. We want Keyla. Keyla is Creed's. That means we need to make it work with Creed as well.

"Everything all right?" Creed asks tossing a bottle of liquid onto the bed. "Second thoughts?"

I shake my head. "Just doing a gut-check."

"And?"

"S'all good. I'm all in."

There's that uneven smirk again. Funny, I've never seen it when he interacts with other people. Knowing it's a private smile warms something deep in the center of my chest. I may not know him well, but I think getting to know him will be worth the adventure.

When he steps in front of me, he grips my hips and lowers

his chin. He's got height on me but doesn't tower over me like Brant and Hawk. I'm glad about that.

"What are you thinking, Bear? Hard and hot or letting the burn build?"

"Door number two," I say with a chuckle. "I've seen your hard and hot and I don't think my ass can take it. It's been a long while since I've been with a male."

He grins. "I'll try not to break you."

I slide my fingers under the flap of his shirt and check out the wide line of symbology running from his shoulder down to his hip. "This is fucking spank. What does it mean?"

"It's the royal lineage of the Thornebane family."

I trace a few of the whorls of ink, pinch the tightened peak of his nipple, and continue my exploration southward. "No body hair. Is that a natural thing or do you manscape?"

"Natural. Most Guardian classed fae are bare-skinned. Is that a plus or a minus?"

"On you? Definitely a plus. You're a well-put-together male."

"I could say the same."

He hasn't moved his hands from my hips, but as my caress drops, I take a moment to stop and study his cock bobbing between us. "Very well-put-together."

Forcing myself to give up the view of his cock, I lift my gaze. His dark eyes are turbulent, filled with questions I don't understand.

I suppose if everyone and everything I love was taken from me and I was forced to live alone and tormented for years, I'd be a little leery too. "Whatever it is, going forward, I've got your back. You don't know me yet, but I'm someone you can count on."

In answer to that, he steps closer. Our rigid cocks are trapped between our bodies as his hold shifts and he pulls us together. His hands splay up my back and then his lips brush mine.

Unlike when I kiss Keyla, there's no gentlemanly impulse with Creed. The moment his mouth seals over mine, something inside me unlocks, and then it's on.

As crazy as it is, this man is my mate.

He's a fucking prince of the fae realm and if I have anything to do about it, he'll be the next King of Dornte.

I'm not sure what he does with his mind gift but as his tongue plunges into my mouth, I get erotic flashes of him pinning me to the mattress, of him spinning me and fucking me hard as I grip the footboard of the bed, and then of him throwing me onto my back and spreading my legs to pump wildly inside me.

"Fuck me," I gasp, the sensations overwhelming.

"That's the idea," he says. "Any of those previews look good?"

"All of them, your pick. Where do you want me?"

A few racing heartbeats later I'm on my back, sprawled across his monstrous mattress and he's on all fours, draping his body over me. His mouth reclaims mine and his hair falls forward, enclosing us within a curtain of silver silk.

I'm lost in the sweep of his tongue and the smooth glide of his skin against mine.

I spread my thighs and pull him tight to my body, so our hard cocks rub together between us.

We both curse and the scent of his need is ratcheting up at an incredible rate. "I smell your hunger. Take from me whatever you need to soothe that ache."

His hips rock, undulating against mine as his tongue pillages and plunders my mouth and our pecs rub. The electric connection of skin-on-skin... the friction of hard cocks rubbing... the frenzied wet heat of our mouths consuming one another...

I'm dizzy with drink and lust, my chest pumping and my fingers gripping his hair.

"Fuck. You need to get inside me before I die." I spread my thighs and he rises onto his knees between my legs. Reaching for that bottle, he squirts out a puddle of liquid, reaches down, and I prop up my hips.

The liquid is cold, but his fingers are warm. "This has a bit of tingle to it too."

His finger rims my anus over and over, pushing the lube inside me. The air vibrates with the growl of my bear as he pleads for more. Damn, it's been a long time for me since being with another guy. The way Creed works me in, I sense that's not the same for him.

Closing my eyes, I arch my back, hissing as he takes hold of my cock too. "Okay. I could get used to this."

And then the hand job is gone and he slides off the bed. "Change of plans. I want to stand and have better access to thrust."

Well, who would argue with that?

The room shifts as he grabs my ankles and swivels me across the mattress. At the edge of the bed, he flips me onto my belly. The moment my feet find purchase on the floor I realize the height of this huge bed is perfect.

I'm piked at the waist and my chassis is at the exact height for him to have easy access.

"You ready for me?"

"Yeah," I choke out. "Go for it."

The pressure of his cock against my ass ignites an urge to push back. I want this. Now that we're here, my blood is pounding.

This is my mate. And he's not a gentleman.

The penetration is swift, the sting substantial, the feeling shockingly intense. My unused body struggles to accommodate the thickness of him but there are no complaints. He's hard and thick and thanks to that lube he spread around, he's got a wicked slide going on.

"Fuck yes." I fist the comforter with both hands and use my

considerable strength to brace myself. "Mark me hard because then it's my turn and my bear and I won't go easy on you."

"Something to look forward to, then."

"Without a doubt."

His hold on my hips constricts with brutal force. I'll have ten little round bruises from his fingers to remind me of this later, but I don't give a shit.

Holy hell that liquid lube of his is tingling like a mother-fucker and zinging sensation straight to my balls.

Creed groans and gets his groove on.

Yanking my hips to meet his powerful thrusts, he drives into me without apology. It's rough the first few times and I wonder if a cock as hard and powerful as his can actually burst right through me.

Then, as the lube slicks his cock more and my inner work-ings relax, things get easier.

His breath bursts out of him in primitive grunts every time he buries himself fully.

With my bear's strength Creed doesn't knock me forward when he thrusts, he buries deep and withdraws. It's punishing and there's no doubt in my mind that he's marking me as his own.

Good, because that's what he'll get as soon as he's done. I drop my forehead to the blanket and absorb the moment. Erotic scents coalesce and fill the air: our arousal, the sex we've already had with Keyla, and the sweat of being thoroughly fucked.

Creed's thrusts push my cock against the mattress with every in and out. The silky softness of the comforter against the hard shaft of my arousal is soooo good.

"What's a girl gotta do to get in on this?" Keyla asks, grinning from the footboard.

There's a brief moment when I stiffen, feeling like a horny teenager caught fucking around by his parents. I'm washed with panic and then guilt and then embarrassment. Unbeknownst to us, she walked in and watched me getting the full Brokeback treatment.

Her tongue peeks out and glides across her lips. "A girl takes a moment to pass out in the afterglow of a great orgasm and the party rages on without her."

"On the bed, Little Wolf," Creed says, his voice husky and breathy. "On your back, legs open."

Keyla grins and does exactly as she's told.

"Bear, you haven't been inside our girl yet this round. Climb in and I'll finish inside you up there."

I chuckle at myself because I take his suggestion and move just as quickly as Keyla did. I hate to lose the fullness of him inside me, but this is a change of position I'm looking forward to.

Besides, we're not done yet.

Crawling up Keyla's beautiful body, our eyes lock. "Hey, babe. So, this is us now, eh?"

She brushes her fingers through the sweat-damp roots of my hair. "I guess it is. Having fun?"

"Even more now that you're here." I guide my cock through the moist heat of her folds and then ease into her core. A primal part of me knows it's not only Keyla's juices there. I'm slicking myself in Creed's cum as well.

That is excruciatingly carnal.

When I'm buried inside her heat, I close my eyes and absorb the sensation. She wraps her arms around my shoulder and pulls me down for a kiss. I'm distracted by the bliss of having her tongue in my mouth when another round of that tingling lube gets applied to my ass.

I growl and push back against the ministration.

"I'll give you a few strokes to get your fuck on, bear, and then I'm finishing what we started."

"Yes, sir." I make use of my few strokes, tilting my hips and rubbing the crown of my cock against the tender spots inside her. I watch Keyla with avid fascination and learn what she aches for.

This is only my second time inside her and I'll need so much more to learn her every nuance. My bear growls inside me... but, yeah, we're willing to put in the time.

My turn of glide and slide is over too soon.

Creed shifts in behind me and reclaims my ass. Re-entry burns for a bit and he gives me a moment to settle.

Ready to crank this up, Bear?

I push against his position while still kissing Keyla.

Once we start going at it with all three of us, I lose track of where I end, and they begin. It's a mate fucking sandwich and I'm lucky enough to be the middle.

Everything becomes a sexy blur of writhing bodies and if this is my last moment on earth, I can die a happy man. There is too much hunger to make sense of whose hands are where and all the pleasure rushing at me from every angle.

Creed is a machine.

After fucking Keyla to exhaustion on the rug, he's giving me the same treatment on the bed. And really, he's fucking Keyla again now too... only with my cock inside her.

Because it's not me who's thrusting and rocking this mattress, that's all Creed. Each time he slams into me, the force drives me into our girl.

This is one time in life where it's pretty fucking awesome to be stuck in the middle.

Creed commands the rhythm, taking what he needs, giving us both what we want. When Keyla's insides start to grip and tighten around my cock, I grasp the nape of her neck and get ready.

Either Creed senses she's about to detonate or he has really good timing because he opens that mental channel of his and then we're sharing sensations.

Keyla's orgasm explodes through us and I feel the pulsing

spasms of her core radiate through her until she's trembling in my arms. The greedy hunger of her wolf is hot and I moan as my release bears down hard.

"Fuck, fuck, fuck," I growl, pounding forward as my body jerks and then my hips lock. My mind fragments as I spill into her and at the same time feel the pulsing pleasure Keyla feels.

Keyla cries out and arcs her back off the mattress and then it's Creeds turn. He rides out my release and then, once I relax, he takes us home.

Every deep thrust he batters into me, builds his tension. When he can't take it any longer. When his heart is bounding and his legs and abdominals are burning, his release bursts free.

His rough shout echoes across the room and inside our minds. I feel his balls clenching tight, slick, hot cum releasing in waves of satisfaction. Fuck.

Sex with an open mental connection is consuming.

Spent, he collapses onto my back, his heart hammering against my spine. He dismounts and rolls to one side of Keyla and I roll off her and take the other.

"Wow," Keyla finally manages. "I may be new to this, but that was good, right?"

I bark a laugh, my heart still pounding in my temples. "Yes… incredible."

The pride in her smile is so fucking gratifying.

I raise my head to meet Creed's gaze across the sweaty mounds of Keyla's beautiful tits. "I know I said I was going to do you hard right after but that will have to wait. I think I just suffered a coronary."

Creed's grin is smug as fuck. "I'll be around. You can make it up to me when we can both move."

I laugh. "No telling when that might be."

CHAPTER SEVEN

Keyla

The three of us come down from our incredible sex high and I'm more than a little pleased with myself. As I clean up in the bathroom, my wolf is downright prancing. The two of them not only found their pleasure with me, but they also had a side hustle going on while I drifted off.

I finish with the washcloth and rinse it clean, loading it up with hot water for the next taker. When I woke up and saw the two of them hard at it, I thought about leaving them to share that on their own. In the end, I decided I wanted to be part of their first time together.

I'm glad I did.

This is only the beginning of what we can be. I know it. I feel it.

A knock on the living room door brings Rhylan into the outer room. I'm the readiest to receive, so I toss the damp cloth toward the two naked bodies on the bed and close the door behind me.

Striding through the living room of the royal suite, I head toward the dual sofas to find my clothes. "That door was locked. You have a key, I take it."

Rhylan eyes me up and down, his mouth agape. He seems to catch himself and lifts his gaze. "I'm his guard. Of course, I have a key."

I find my underwear and then fish my bra out from the heap of discarded clothing. Once my essentials are covered, I gather the rest of the clothes and walk them back to the bedroom to toss them inside the door.

"You're not shy, I take it?" Rhylan says.

I chuckle at the sarcasm in his tone. "I'm surprised it even registers with you."

"You're surprised I notice you flaunting around naked in front of me? A stranger. You're a princess, for slecking sake. Do you think Creed's mate and future queen of his quadrant should act this way?"

"I see nothing inappropriate. I'm in the private royal quarters. You're the one who let himself in uninvited. A little earlier and you would've interrupted the three of us naked on the rug. Is that me being inappropriate or you?"

He sends me a scathing look and I suspect the stench of fury rolling off him in acrid waves has less to do with me being naked and more to do with me being the one having sex with Creed.

"In our realm," I say, undeterred, "wildlings are so accustomed to shifting around others, we don't give nakedness much thought. I'm sorry you find my body so offensive."

Rounding the end of the sofa, I catch his scent and my wolf stretches. I chuckle. "But you're not completely offended, are you? You like what you see... which is probably even more maddening."

I step in front of him, regarding the mop of blond covering

his expression. He's all about standing out as the queen's biggest and baddest, but he's hiding. He doesn't want to be seen and me being this close brings out the smokey scent of his anxiety.

I tilt my head and try to figure him out. "Maybe we got off on the wrong foot. I'm sorry the searing disrupted what you and Creed had. I'm sorry I upset the balance by worrying it was something violent. Since you are his guard, and therefore ours by extension, I'd like to work on finding common ground."

His jaw flexes as he lifts his head and stares straight at the back wall. "Lines may have gotten blurred but that is between Creed and me. You and I are not friends. You'd do well to stay out of my way and keep your mouth shut about Creed and me fucking around. That info is private and—"

Creed clears his throat, and we turn to find him and Doc standing at the entrance to the room looking like they walked in on something.

Which they did.

Creed's brow tightens in a hard scowl. "If you want to keep it private, maybe you should stop bringing it up."

Doc nods. "All right. Now a few more things make sense. You calling Keyla a bitch. The outburst about her keeping her mouth shut. The lengths you went for him after he fried your noggin."

I nod. "Except I *have* kept my mouth shut. I was concerned for Creed and I spoke to him privately. Rhylan has trust issues."

Rhylan's gaze narrows. He turns to address Creed directly when the door to the outer suites opens and Kotah and his mates come through for the drink and think.

My brother stops and stiffens. His gift likely picked up on the tension in the room. "Sorry, is this a bad time? Should we come back?"

I shake my head and pull on the rest of my clothes. "No. I'm thrilled you're here. Come in. Creed sent Brant's wish list down to the kitchen and we should have our supplies shortly. Come. Make yourselves at home."

I turn back to Creed. *Is it all right that I welcome them? Am I overstepping?*

Not at all. Your family is now my family. They are welcome. And honestly. We could use a gathering of friends. If you'll excuse me a moment, I'd like to speak to Rhylan privately.

Of course... and Creed? I smell the pain of his rejection. His frustration with me being here is more personal than it is professional. He's hurting.

His brows drop as if he disagrees, but I know what I smell. Rhylan isn't happy about me being here but it has little to do with keeping his prisoner under his thumb.

Creed hasn't opened up to me about what happened between the two of them, but by the heated daggers the two of them are throwing off at one another, it was more than physical exertion to pass the time...

Or at least it grew to be.

Rhylan

My entire body is vibrating. That bitch has the gall to speak about me and Creed while she still wears his mark on her flesh? And what's worse, he wasn't enough for her, so she roped in her old boyfriend so now my dark and haunted prince is fucking *both* of them?

My dragon paces wildly within me, my skin crawling with the olfactory offense of their scents.

My fire burns hot with the need to fix this.

Creed isn't theirs. He's *mine.*

I see the focused look passing between them and curse. They're linked and having private conversations. Mind fae save that connection for only the most intimate relationships.

Another thing she gets that I never had.

My eyes flip to dragon gold and burn with the fractured vision of my animal self. I need to get out of here.

Someone curses and I swing my gaze. They're looking at me. The quint. Creed. His mates.

Everyone needs to stop looking at me!

"Rhy, what's wrong?" Creed's concern washes over me like a balm. Then he shifts to step between me and his wolf bitch. No. He's not concerned about *me*.

It's *her* he wants to protect.

"He's losing control of his dragon," the Wolf King snaps. "Calli, take Keyla into the other room. She's upsetting his beast."

Brant positions himself between me and the ladies retreating toward Honor's suite. "Can I point out dragons don't make for good house pets?"

A joke? My life is imploding and they're making fun of me? My control evaporates behind a blast of fury so great, the man I am is rendered speechless.

My dragon, though… my dragon has something to say. "Leave. You have no right to be here."

My voice comes out strained and warbled with my dragon's power. There's no reining it in.

"They're here by my invitation," Creed snaps. "What the fuck is wrong with you?"

"They ruined everything." My dragon's hiss vibrates, filling the room. A buzz hums through me, echoing in my head. "*I* protect you. *I* care for you. Not them."

Creed points to his bedroom. "How about a bit of privacy. For fuck's sake, Rhy, you're losing your shit."

"I'm losing everything. I'm losing *you*," I snap, rushing him. With the strength of my dragon behind me, I lift him off his feet and pin him to the wall.

He jerks his head to the side, but I catch his chin, bringing his attention back to me. "Mine."

Dropping my mouth, I extend my incisors and bite.

Creed cries out.

There's no stopping this. He *is* mine. My hard, hot length spears into his abdomen. I rub the front of his pants, finding his response.

Like it or not, he wants what we have.

With a clawed swipe, I slice through the front of his pants and free that erection.

"Mine…" I hiss against the flesh of his neck and his blood seeps into my mouth. It's warm and sinfully delicious as it hits my tongue. That exquisite flavor is the answer to my claim.

Dark spice bleeds from my skin as I grind against him and my mating scent releases. I moan as I press against him. "Mine."

~

Doc

"Oh fuck. This isn't good." The dragon has Creed pinned to the wall and is dry humping him in a very obvious display of staking his claim. The thing is, I can't tell if the dreamy haze in Creed's eyes is him getting off on the whole thing or being lulled into some kind of dragon fuck trance.

"What should we do?" I turn and catch the stunned gazes of Keyla and the entire quint. "Do we try to stop it? Do we risk having a pissed dragon in the middle of the castle?"

Keyla gathers herself quickly and seems to be the only one with an answer. She's wearing that focused look she gets when she and Creed talk cranium to cranium. "He's all right. We'll let them have a moment."

She rakes her fingers through her long, chestnut hair and

rolls her eyes at Calli. "It seems my questions about Rhylan and our mating have been answered."

Calli tilts her head, to improve her view of the show. "In a big way."

Keyla chuckles. "Okay, you guys go ahead and set things up for our meeting of the minds out here. Doc and I will see if we can move this into the bedroom and get it sorted."

Sorted? We've got a dragon crazed with lust, anger, and frustration and she thinks we should welcome him into our mating? "Am I missing something? Since when were we considering a fourth?"

She looks up at me and frowns. "Since Creed invited *my* significant other into our fated mating and I realized Rhylan was more to him than a jailor and a tormentor."

I shake my head, my bear rising inside me. "You sure that's all it is? Seems to me, you're rounding yourself up quite a stable of studs, Princess."

The slap to my cheek stings my heart far more than my face.

Her wolf lets off a long, low growl of warning.

"That was uncalled for, Bear. You've been grumbling beneath the surface for days. Look around. We're here to unite two realms. We've been given a chance to live extraordinary lives. I understand you're protective of what we have, but I need you to expand your perspective. I want you here. I love you. I want what's best for you and me and Creed and both fucking worlds, so get your head out of your very fine ass and realize this is about more than the two of us living happily ever after."

I stretch my jaw and rub at the scruff of my cheek. Wow, she's pissed. She f-bombed me and everything. My pretty little princess is taking off the gloves.

Honestly, the fire in her eyes is too fucking sexy.

My girl has fight I didn't even know about.

Dayam, girl.

"Well, all righty then. Sometimes bears spout off before they think. Consider me set straight, slugger."

Her gaze narrows. "Are you laughing at me?"

"Not as much as I'm loving at you. Come on, give me another little spanking. I deserve it."

She rolls her eyes. "You're not half as cute as you think you are. Now, help me get them into the bedroom before things get more awkward for Creed."

Awkward?

Creed is a vision of male ecstasy. With his head kicked back, his silver hair flowing to his bare chest, and a look of tortured pleasure etched on his face, I'm not sure *awkward* is the word I'd use to describe him.

Chin held high, the smooth column of Creed's throat is mostly covered by the dragon's mouth. Rhylan is drinking from his neck and palming him roughly. The front of Creed's pants are shredded and falling open.

"*Fuck.* That is erotic as hell. Anyone else throwing wood like a Scotsman in a caber toss competition?" Cue the rising hands of Brant, Kotah, Jaxx, and Hawk. "Good to know I'm not alone."

"On second thought," Keyla says. "Let's leave them right where they are, and we can all head across to your suite for a bit."

"Yeah," Jaxx says, adjusting the front of his ripped jeans. "A little distance is probably a good idea."

Hawk scans the bulge pushing at Jaxx's fly and arches a brow. "You need a hand with that, Puss?"

Jaxx grins. "If you're offerin', I'm acceptin'."

Calli shakes her head and smiles at Keyla. "Okay, on third thought, I'll take my four across the hall and ride this out. You four handle your recent development and we'll regroup in a while, hopefully when everyone is level and sated."

And with that, the phoenix and her quint make a heated and hasty exit.

Keyla

I close and lock the door, chuckling to myself. Over the past three months, there have been dozens of moments when Calli and the quint, either on a whole or a few members at a time, have been in the middle of some kind of sexual exploitation when Dillan and I walked in.

It got to be a bit of a game, guessing what we might stumble into.

It seems our life might be following the same path.

And still, the quint gets to share in the sexual exploits. I'm happy for them.

Flopping on the couch, I lean back and pat the cushion beside me. Doc sinks down beside me and the weight of his body on the cushions tilts me toward him.

He takes my hand and kisses my cheek. "Sorry about the pissing match."

The two of us watch the two of them and I shrug. "Eyes forward, Bear. It's our only way through this."

He chuckles. "I gotta say, eyes forward right now is no sacrifice. Fuck they're hot."

I nod, utterly enthralled by the prince and dragon porn show. Sure, we could give them privacy but Rhylan's dragon has to learn that despite him staking his claim, Creed is ours too.

It doesn't take long before Creed's breathing is coming in short, quick gasps and he squeezes his eyes shut. His release hits in a rough, hard gasp of breath, and his body shudders.

Rhylan strokes him off and swipes his tongue over the punctures in his neck. Then he lifts his hand and growls as he licks Creed's release off his hand.

A moment later, the energy in the air shifts. By the shattered look on Rhy's face as he eases back, his dragon descended, leaving the man to face the consequences.

Being wildlings ourselves, Dillan and I have both been-there-done-that. Losing control of our animal side happens to all of us.

It doesn't always leave you mated to three other people but hey, if you're doing something, might as well do it big.

The minute he meets Creed's gaze the dragon gets panicky. "Slecking hell… Creed, I'm…" He turns and sees us there and curses again.

Creed looks like he's in shock. He glances from Rhy, to us, and then, without a word, he turns and disappears into the bedroom. The *boom* of the bathroom door slamming echoes through the suite.

Rhylan stiffens and closes his eyes.

"It's not as bad as it must seem," I say, offering him an olive branch. "We've all been there over the past few days and we understand what you're going through. What you need to do now is not overreact."

Rhylan's face twists in pained horror. "Not overreact? She'll kill me. She'll kill my brother. And when our alpha learns of this, our family name will be forfeit and the Silverwings will be erased from the ancient scrolls. My mother will be nameless."

There's a lot in that statement I don't understand, but what's clear is that, given a level-headed choice, Rhylan wouldn't have chosen to mate Creed.

"You must love him, or your dragon wouldn't have gotten so aggressively protective about losing him."

"Caring about someone and thinking they're getting a raw deal is a far cry from wanting to mate him and two strangers and sentencing your family to death and ruin."

There's a knock on the door and Rhylan looks like a spooked horse about to bolt.

I stand and raise a hand. "Yes, who is it?"

"It's Vikarus. I need to speak with my brother. Is he in there?"

Rhylan's eyes widen, and he looks like he might pass out. "He can't come in here," he whispers. "I'm covered in Creed's sweat and..."

He looks at the hand he used to prime Creed's release and I think he might be sick.

I point to the bedroom. "We'll take care of this. You calm down and go clean up."

CHAPTER EIGHT

Creed

Gripping the edge of the sink, I stare at myself in the reflection of the mirror. The puncture marks on the side of my neck are red and raw. Fuck. I didn't know dragons dropped fang and did that shit. Rhylan certainly never did before now.

A shiver racks me as the sensation of the penetration floods back in a rush—it's a lightning strike straight to my crotch.

I close my eyes and try to breathe through the tightening in my chest. Did that actually happen?

The swing of the door has my attention shifting across the mirror to the bathroom behind me.

Rhy stands there, pale and anxious. "I… I didn't mean to do that… I'm sorry."

I lock my legs, tighten my grip on the countertop, and clench my jaw. If I move, I'll take him to the ground and not in a good way.

"I lost control of my dragon…"

No shit. That became apparent the moment he nailed me to the wall and made me his sex toy juice box.

He curses and sweeps his blond bangs out of his face. He looks wrecked. His eyes are still the gold of his wildling side and brimming with moisture. "I shouldn't have—I *wouldn't* have if I had any control."

I believe him, but it doesn't change anything. Especially if what I think happened, actually did happen.

"Did you claim me as your mate?"

He dips his chin, his eyes locked on mine and half-masted. "I'm sorry."

A million emotions spin within the vortex inside me, not the least of which are fury and betrayal. "You stole my choice. Out of anyone in this fucking castle, you know how I suffer because of people taking over my life. You see everything that's been taken from me and yet you fucking claim me in a rage... and in front of my mates and their family?"

He staggers back, his hand pressed against his heart.

"Now I have to go out there and explain to them that not only were we fucking around but Keyla and Dillan are now bound to a hot-tempered idiot dragon who they don't know and who's playing for the wrong team."

Fire flashes in his eyes. "I'm more than my appointment to a violent bitch. I'm a man who happens to be duty-bound to serve the crown regardless of my personal convictions."

"And you mated your prisoner!" I push off the counter to turn to him. "How does that work into your duty roster? Do you think that will fly? I'm not a wildling, but I'm pretty fucking sure that scent you released marked me, didn't it?"

He winces.

"And now any wildling or fae with heightened smell will think I belong to you."

"You *do* belong to me." He storms farther into the bathroom and slams the door shut behind him. "That decision has been made. We can pretend it didn't happen, but a dragon's claim is a lock. You are *mine*."

"And do *I* get a say in that?"

A cruel smile curves his mouth. "You got your say. Your blood sang to me and your heart was mine. It's your fault my scent released. If your response to my advance had been different, the claiming wouldn't have kicked in and nothing would've taken hold."

Fuck me. "Bullshit. You're backpedaling."

He shakes his head. "I'm not. I didn't mean for it to happen, but your reaction gave the process the go-ahead, and here we are."

I chuff. "Am I supposed to believe you? Fuck, Rhy. How many times have you lied to me over the past two years? Now I'm supposed to believe you about something as important as this?"

He paces forward, his wiry frame rigid and tense. "I couldn't tell you everything, obviously, but I never lied to you about anything personal."

I get up in his grill, my chest heaving. I've got a few inches on him and it gives me a slight edge to back him the hell down. "Nothing personal? Like my sister escaping imprisonment or my mother being dead? Nothing personal, like that?"

He has the decency to drop his gaze. "I meant personal about us."

I shake my head. "What *us*, Dragon? You snuck into my room a couple of nights a month and we fucked."

"It was more than that and you know it."

"Do I? We drew a line—enemies with benefits."

"And it got away on us."

"When? Once you saw that I had a chance at something real? The universe places a potential queen at my side and gives me the support I need to reclaim my life, *then* you move on me?"

"It wasn't planned."

"Does that change anything? We're still mated. Fuck, Rhy, how do I face them? Keyla must be horrified. You injected yourself into our mating and jacked me off in front of her and her family. One of which is the king of the fucking *Human Realm!* How do you think that will go over?"

"Can I answer that?" Keyla cracks the door open.

I turn on my heel, too unsteady to face her. My cheeks flush hot and my stomach squirrels. "I'm so, fucking sorry, Keyla. I don't even know what to say."

"It happened. It's done. Don't be sorry. The important thing now is how we handle it. Vikarus is gone for now but we need to get Rhylan cleaned up and figure out how to mask his scent on you."

Shaking my head, I turn to meet her gaze. It's as strong and steady as always. "How? How could you see what you saw and not be thrown? I'm mortified. Your family must be horror-struck."

She snorts. "Hardly. My family found the entire exchange as carnal as I did. They excused themselves to go get naked and work off the effects of your mating in their suite. They'll be back once they're sated."

I rub a hand over my mouth, my heart pounding. She genuinely doesn't seem angry or hurt. "I don't understand. Maybe I don't know anything about what mating means in your world, but you should be furious with both of us."

The deep timbre of Doc's chuckle precedes him coming through the door and entering the mix. "Try not to assign logic to her, my man. The females in our realm will turn the tables on you every time."

"And how do you feel about this, Bear?"

"What does it matter?" Rhylan snaps, scowling. "It doesn't affect them. I didn't mate them. They're not part of this."

Dillan chuckles again and leans his broad shoulder against the doorframe, filling the exit. "That's where you're wrong,

Dragon. Like it or not, it's the four of us now. You might've claimed Creed as your own, but he wasn't on the market. The universe gave him to Keyla, and you and I were added into the mix."

Rhy doesn't seem to agree, so I hold out my hand to Keyla and pull her to my hip. "Keyla and I are together and even though it's early days, it's amazing. We're well-matched and our feelings grow deeper with every exchange."

By the light in her eyes, I earned a few bonus points with that declaration of affection.

I shift my focus back to Rhy. "Mating me means mating us. Dillan and I had this discussion and it bears repeating. Keyla and I are destined for great things and although neither of us expected it, we are embracing it. Dillan and I are working on building a relationship and I will be as much his mate as I am hers. I'm not sure what you expected, but I'm not an individual —I'm part of a throuple."

Keyla chuckles at the use of the word she introduced to me only days ago.

I wrap my arm around her shoulder and bend to kiss the top of her head. Having her close and breathing her in soothes me. She has quickly become my source of strength and support.

I hate the rejection I see in Rhylan's eyes but there's no benefit in pretending our situation is anything but what it is. "Having your dragon claim me complicates things, but I understand how it happened."

Keyla places a hand on my bare abdomen and smiles up at me. "The three of us learned over the past week that our future won't be what we initially envisioned, and that's okay."

"If we work on it together, it'll be more," Doc says, offering me a nod. "Different, and more."

Rhylan shakes his head. "You're talking like this is something I want. It isn't. I don't. My dragon's possession got the better of me and now... slecking hell, I don't know how to fix it."

"The first thing is to get you across the hall and washed up." Keyla breathes deep and shakes her head. "Doc and I will run interference to get you back to your suite without a confrontation with Vikarus. You need to shower and get into clean clothes that don't smell like sex with Creed. I'll speak to Lukas about suppressing the mating scent."

Rhylan's icy gaze narrows on her and the intensity of his glare raises the hair on my neck. "Why would you help me?"

She lifts her shoulders and winks. "Because we're mates now and that's what mates do."

~

Keyla

On the way back from relocating Rhylan into his suite, I knock on the door to The Auburn Suite down the hall. "All clear. Come over when you're ready."

With that, I turn, and Doc opens the door to Creed and Honor's royal suite. Closing ourselves in, I lean against the back of the door and close my eyes. Water is running in the distance and I feel bad for Creed and the upheaval of what he's going through—again.

"Anything I can do, babe?"

"How about a bear hug. I could use your strength."

Doc gathers me against his chest and wraps his arms around me. "Have I told you lately that I think you're beautiful and the most amazing person I know?"

I nuzzle against the scruff of his jaw and breathe him in. "No, but I'm listening."

His chest bounces against my cheek. "I'm sorry I grumble at times. It's not you. It's a bear thing."

I know it is. Still, sometimes it bugs me. "I need your support, Doc. There are so many things changing so quickly that I need you as my foundation. Don't ever underestimate your importance to me."

"I'll try. And I'll try to be more of a team player, but I still might need some alone time with you. My bear and I need you to ourselves, too."

I close my eyes as he strokes the back of my hair and I sink into his hold. It strikes me that this is the first quiet time we've had together since it all began. There was our mating, but that was rushed and filled with pressure to join up with Creed and get into the city.

It's nice to have nothing waiting for us.

For this moment, there is me and my bear.

"Calli says it's all about balance and each mate expressing what they need. I'll never object to you wanting one-on-one time with me. I need that too. Don't ever think I'm filling a corral and forgot my first stud."

He chuckles. "First stud. I like that. I think I'll get a t-shirt made."

I ease back to smile up at him. "I love you, Bear."

He meets my lips with a simple kiss of warmth and affection. "I love you, too."

Doc

By the time Brant and the quint make their way back for the Drink and Think, Keyla seems to be firing at full power again and I'm glad to have been the one to give her the recharge. I forget sometimes she's not as invincible as she seems.

Life in the spotlight of a realm taught her how to handle adversity with poise and grace. From the outside, it looks like things don't rattle her, but deep down, she's still a young woman with the weight of two worlds pressing down on her.

As she welcomes our brothers and gets everyone set up for our strategy session, I head into the bedroom to check on Creed. The guy has always been clean, but no one could take that long in the shower.

The bedroom wall panel is open and Creed is standing in the hidden closet. With both hands gripped on the hanging rail above, he's got his eyes closed and seems lost in thought, he doesn't hear me join him or at least doesn't acknowledge it.

Wearing only a towel wrapped around his hips, the patchy white scars on his back catch me by surprise.

I've never seen him with his shirt off. Even when we were fucking he had his shirt on... unbuttoned and covering his back.

The damage has long since healed, but it just goes to show, you never know what someone's been through. With that in mind, I knock on the door frame and give him a second as he jumps and throws a shirt on.

"Sorry," I say, leaning on the frame. "I didn't mean to disturb you."

He shakes his head. "It's fine. I'm fine."

"Are you? No one would blame you if you're not."

"I would." He pulls a pair of slacks off a hanger and steps into them commando. Then he gestures for me to unblock the doorway. "I've tarnished my impression on your family as much as I can stand."

"Nah, we're not like that. No one would think badly if you pass on tonight considering the day's events."

He buttons up his dress shirt and tucks the tails into his pants before grabbing a belt and some socks from the dresser drawers. "And what then? Should I hide in a closet for the rest of the night?"

I shrug. "What one man calls hiding, another might consider stepping back and gaining clarity. Keyla said something to me just now and I think it applies to your situation too. She said, our happiness is about balance and each of us expressing what we need. If you need a minute, take it. We've got you."

He sits on the chair beside the dresser and pulls his socks on before standing and checking himself in the massive floor-to-ceiling mirror. "I appreciate it, Bear. I do. I just feel like my life is out of my control and I need to assert myself where I can."

"Anything I can do to help?"

He extends his arm and I mirror the gesture and clamp his wrist as he grasps mine. "You're doing it. Thank you."

Before we leave the bedroom, he straightens and holds his arms to the sides. "How do I look?"

"Dapper and sexy."

That earns me a sultry smile. "Why Mr. Baskins, are you flirting with me?"

"In my defense, you're looking spank and I'll be the only one out there who knows you're free-balling."

He chuckles. "It's no wonder Human Realm slang and idioms are such a craze here. You guys say the most outrageous things."

"It's true, not outrageous. You're swinging loose and long and that's sexy as fuck."

A flush hits his cheeks. "Thanks for saying so, Bear. You're a good guy."

CHAPTER NINE

Keyla

*I*t's hard to miss how long it's taking for Creed to join us. Doc went in to check on him and still nothing. I'm about to excuse myself and go in there when the two of them finally emerge.

Creed's a little dressy for the occasion, but I'm not complaining. A male in slacks and a pressed shirt pushes my buttons. And the way his broad shoulders taper down to his slim, belted waist is breathtaking.

"So, it's going well then?" Kotah asks, reaching around my shoulder to give me a side hug. "Between the prince and you, I mean. I have no doubts about Doc. He's a solid guy and loves you. Creed seems to be following his lead though—falling in love with you, I mean."

My two guys are sticking close to one another and Doc takes him over to the bar. What was a butler's cart with a few bottles has been upgraded to Jaxx's specifications and is now a full-on party bar.

I lay my head on Kotah's shoulder and try not to worry.

Doc's got him. "I think it's harder for him. He's an alpha male, right? The would-be king. He lost his crown and his family and his say in life and then the moment things shift, something like the thing with Rhylan happens and he feels like his footing is more gravel than ground."

Kotah nods. "I know exactly how that feels."

"Out of all of us, you would know best, My King."

Kotah arches a brow and chuffs.

Creed gets served by Jaxx and leaves Doc chatting with Brant to join us. He's standing tall and lifts his chin, but he reeks of embarrassment and shame. "I must apologize," he says, swallowing. "For Rhylan and... what happened. Keyla's been gracious about it but—"

Kotah squeezes Creed's shoulder. "All I care about is that you treat my sister well and she's happy. What happens behind closed doors—even if others happen to witness it—won't sway our opinion of you."

Calli snorts, joining us with a plate of finger foods. "If it makes you feel better, our quint had a similarly embarrassing event in our early days."

Kotah chuckles. "Which one?"

I grin at Creed. "There are too many to count."

"True story," Calli says. "I was referring to our first naked nacho night."

Hawk and Lukas come in the door in time to hear her and Hawk rolls his eyes. "Oh, fuck. Why would you bring that up?"

"Bring what up?" Brant asks, loping over. "Come on. Share with the rest of the class."

Calli grins. "If I'm not mistaken, Prince Creed is embarrassed—"

"—mortified," Creed corrects.

"—mortified," Calli says, "about the public display of private affairs. I think we should tell him about our first naked nacho night and ease his misery."

"Then I'll need a drink." Hawk heads toward the bar. "And before the night devolves into whatever drunk debacle we have in store, yes, Lukas masked Creed's scent off Rhylan and yes, he can do the same for Creed."

Jaxx lifts a bottle at the bar. "The Phoenix Quint, putting out one fire at a time. Well done, Lukas."

Everyone offers Lukas a round of thanks.

"And what have we discovered about the blood witch?" Creed asks.

Lukas fields that one himself. "I brought a team of FCO enforcers through the rift and have the building under surveillance. It might take a day or two, but we'll know more then."

"What about your beacon buzz?" Doc asks. "Is that telling us anything we need to know?"

Creed checks with me and I shake my head. "It's there but not going haywire. For now, it seems like we're on standby."

"Then back to naked nachos," Calli says.

Since no one jumps into it, I begin the tale. "So, Kotah and his mates had just arrived at the palace. My father's health was failing, and Mother was appalled Kotah mated a commoner who didn't know what it meant to be a wildling or a royal."

"That's me," Calli says, waving a skewer of meat. "I tried to make a good impression, but the Prima wasn't impressed. In fact, she hated me."

Jaxx chuckles. "Sorry, kitten, I'm not sure you can use a past tense on that."

Calli chuckles. "You're probably right. She still hates me."

"Her loss," Hawk says, returning with a tumbler of whiskey in hand. "At that time, I was in another part of town at a fae conference. It was before I consummated our mating and I was not only the odd man out, but Brant also didn't trust me and convinced Jaxx that for the sake of the realm, they should start snooping into my life to expose me as a corrupt traitor."

Brant's chuckling now. "So, Jaxx and I thought while Hawk was gone, a drunken night of debauchery was in order."

"That part of the evening was going very well," Kotah adds, smiling. "We'd been drinking all night, playing various adult games Jaxx came up with, leaving us less than presentable."

I laugh picturing it all unfolding. "But earlier that day, Kotah had asked me to soften up our mother and bring her around. Not knowing what they were up to, I convinced her to give Kotah and his mates another chance and get to know them."

"And around that time," Hawk says. "I found out about Brant and Jaxx thinking the worst of me, so I flew back to the palace in a rage. I stormed into the suite and fists started flying."

Kotah rolls his eyes. "So, there we are, Brant naked and spraying Hawk's blood across the décor, Jaxx—"

"—also naked," Calli adds.

Jaxx snorts. "Now, now. My male bits were covered by a lovely little apron."

Kotah laughs. "Yes, they were. Until he got back fisted and was sprawled out cold over the arm of a sofa with his apron flipped up around his hips. Calli was heaving her guts out over the kitchen sink, in her lacy underthings, and Keyla picked that moment to escort our mother into the suite to show her who we really are."

Calli laughs. "Which, who are we kidding, kinda *is* who we really are."

"Yeah, baby," Jaxx says holding up his drink.

"My point is," I say, taking Creed's hand in mine. "Whether it's crazy antics or mortifyingly embarrassing moments or ridiculously inappropriate comments, there's nothing we can't handle in this patchwork family."

"No judgment," Kotah says. "You are part of this family now. You can't shock us and nothing that happened with Rhylan will change the fact that you belong here with Keyla."

"And in a way, it's kinda proof that you're exactly where

you're supposed to be," Jaxx says, tipping back his glass. "And what man hasn't gotten a hand job in front of a room full of people?"

Doc and Lukas raise their hands.

Brant laughs. "Aw, that's too bad, boys. Don't be sad. You're both young and reasonably good-looking. There's still hope for you."

Creed

Keyla and Doc's family is the strangest kind of wonderful. They are inappropriate and funny and genuinely enjoy one another. After an hour of eating and talking about their realm and our plans, I finally let the fiasco with Rhylan go and enjoy myself.

"No, that's bullshit," Brant says, laughing a while later. "If jaguars took over the world, they'd have us all sunning ourselves and swimming."

"Or in your case sinking," Hawk says.

Brant lifts his glass to toast his mate. "No. If it came down to living like one species, everyone should live like bears. Eat when you want. Sleep when you want. And most importantly, kill people in the woods when you want."

Calli laughs. "I think we've killed more than our fair share of people in the woods."

Brant grins. "See. We're well on the way. You'd all be great bears."

Kotah and Jaxx come back from the kitchen with two trays of chicken nachos. Both of them are wearing guilty expressions and I wonder what we missed. The wildings seem to understand immediately.

It's only me, Calli, and Lukas that seem to be on the outside of the joke.

"Seriously?" Doc says, rolling his eyes. "We're out here starving and the two of you are sexing it up in the kitchen?"

Calli gives the nachos a sideways glance. "Where were these during the sexing."

Jaxx laughs. "Still in the oven. Trust me, there's no cross-pollination of anything funky."

Calli laughs and helps herself.

"You're taking their word for it?" Hawk asks arching a brow.

Calli nods. "I'm preggers and hungry. Besides, no trust, no us."

A frisson of energy runs the length of my spine.

I swallow my drink and turn. "Where did you hear that saying?"

Calli looks over at me, chewing a chip. "Pardon?"

"No trust, no us. Is that a Human Realm saying?"

"Not really. My bestie, Riley said it all the time. She's the only one I ever heard say it, why?"

"And Riley is…"

"That's the girl I told you about," Keyla says. "The one we think was from this realm who guided Calli through life to get her ready to become the guardian. We think she was one of your travelers."

Jaxx sets the tray down on the stone coffee table and straightens. "Finding Riley and discovering what happened to her is one of our primary reasons for being here. Whoever she was, we all owe her a debt."

The hazy numbness of alcohol has taken hold, but I fight off the mind fuzz and try to make sense of that. "What made you think she is a traveler?"

"Because after she was physically killed in our realm, she kept talking to me," Calli says. "At first, I thought it was a grieving thing and I was manifesting or projecting or something but as time passed, she knew too much about my mating and opening the rift."

Keyla adjusts on the sofa beside me and reaches for some food. "Jaxx's mom researched which of the fae species in this realm might be able to not only observe but inhabit a person in our realm, but we didn't get far."

Jaxx nods. "Our records are out of date on what the species on this side of the rift can do."

"And how long did you know Riley?" I ask.

"Almost twelve years," Calli says. "She found me when I first ran away and was living on the streets. She took care of me. She taught me how to fight and kept me out of trouble and, in the end, she was the catalyst to bring me and the guys together. We figure she was part of the program Laryssa mentioned for keeping tabs on us but was working for the good guys."

I scrub a hand over my face my heart racing. "The traveler program allows certain fae species to observe events in the other realm, but they wouldn't be able to manifest there and stay for over a decade. That's a different skill altogether."

"Different how?" Hawk asks.

I hold up my finger to the avian and ignore the question for the moment. I need to keep my train of thought on the tracks. "You said this Riley girl continued to speak to you after her human host was killed."

Calli nods. "What does that mean to you?"

"A lot." I get up and jog toward the door. When I step out into the hall, I'm relieved it's Rhylan guarding the door and not Vik. The guy frowns but I don't have time for another round of oops I'm a hot-headed dragon.

"When Honor was caught and recaptured, where was she found? Did you track her activity? Do you know what she did during her time while she was free?"

He glances down the hall before throwing me a glare. "Are you trying to get me killed?"

"No. You're doing a fine job of that on your own."

The two of us standoff until I step back and sweep my hand into the suite. "Come inside."

"Pass. The last time I was in there with you people my life was ruined."

"That was your doing, not theirs. Now, inside. Please, this is important."

Rhy straightens and curses, giving in. Inside the door, he stops dead and stands at attention. "Fine. I'm inside. What do you want?"

"I want you to answer my questions. Where was Honor when you recaptured her and what had she been doing during her escape from Laryssa?"

"Why do you need to know?"

I shove him and slam him against the back of the door. "Stop being such a stubborn prick and answer the fucking question. When my sister was recaptured, where did they find her? StoneHaven? She was in StoneHaven, wasn't she?"

"What if she was?"

I grip his shirt with both hands and lean in until we're nose to nose. "Drop the asshole act for once in your fucking life. I told you, this is important."

His lip curls up in a snarl. "Not an act."

I clench my hand into a fist and am swinging back when Kotah catches my wrist and a warm rush of calming energy washes over me. It stops the drunken swirl in my head and helps a lot.

"Patience might be a more productive approach," Kotah says. "Perhaps if you tell us what you're working out, we can help."

I draw a deep breath and exhale. Releasing my fist, I hold up my hands to Rhy and step back. "Your assumption about a traveler possessing your friend Riley is flawed. It doesn't work that way. Travelers are observers only. The most they can do is take a snapshot of what's happening there and bring that back."

Hawk lifts his chin. "If not a traveler then who or what do you think Riley is?"

"The only species of fae from this realm that could possess a being from your realm would be a mind fae who wields that particular gift. More importantly, only one specific member of my species would have the power behind her to embed herself and withstand the strains of spanning time as you've described."

"All right," Hawk says. "we're all ears. Who are we talking about?"

I peg Rhylan with a look and see the light go off in his mind as he catches up. "Honor."

I nod and meet the confused gazes of the group. "My sister, Honor. I'm pretty sure in the year she escaped Laryssa's captivity, she went to StoneHaven and transferred her consciousness to your realm."

"Slecking hell," Rhylan says, raking his fingers over his forehead and exposing his dazzled expression. "She prepared Calli for her life as the phoenix and initiated the prophecy."

"It's the only thing that makes sense."

"Laryssa was always bragging about what she was up to with Sebastian so she went back, found Calli, and made sure it didn't end her way."

"How?" Calli says. "I don't understand. How could she spend twelve years with me in one year of escape? That makes no sense."

"When you look at time through a linear lens, no," I say. "But Honor and I are more than mind fae, we're guardians. We carry the blooded magic of the ancient crown guardians—the Amberloq warriors."

Keyla steps in to join us by the door. "That was the magic you used to break the hold on the searing to get us back to our human forms?"

"That's right. I lost the ability to access the magic of the

Amberloq when the blood witch cursed me. The soul-searing shook that loose somehow."

"And your sister, Honor?" Calli says. "How would she know to find me and prepare me?"

"The Amberloq guard the timeline. Even though this is our present, for us in the future, this is our past."

Jaxx chuckles. "Am I the only one who wishes we had this conversation before two hours of drinking?"

Brant snorts. "I think I'm getting it. So, your Amber-time-fae-warrior-people from the future knew Calli would rise as the phoenix, but maybe she wasn't ready or tough enough or something, so they have your sister slip back a decade and start training her."

I place a hand on the small of Keyla's back and make our way back toward the sofas. "Exactly. In the royal lineage of our family, the firstborn is a son and the secondborn a daughter. The son is the guardian of the quadrant and the daughter is the guardian of the crown."

"In essence," Rhylan says, "she's the queen of the special forces destined to protect the crown."

"And I take it, your aunt is dead?" Lukas asks. "If Honor has come into her powers and was able to travel back to connect with Calli, she would have to have not only the information about what needed to happen but also the ability to ensure it did."

I look to Rhylan. "At the time of the raid, Valorus escaped with the help of her warriors. It took almost a year for Laryssa to find her and eliminate her."

"And that's right about the time Honor escaped," Doc says. "So they killed Creed's aunt and activated the transfer of power."

Rhylan nods. "Laryssa was unaware of how the Thornebane lineage works. She bound Honor's access to her mind fae powers the same way she did with you but when Valorus was killed, the surge of power disrupted the witch's spell."

I swallow, taking that all in.

Keyla squeezes my hand. "I'm sorry about your aunt. Were you close?"

I meet the sympathetic gazes of the group and shake my head. "No. I barely knew her. My father and she had a falling out when Honor and I were kids. I hadn't seen her since then."

Hawk stands and starts to pace the room. "Aunt Valorus is killed. Honor comes into her powers. The Amberloq inform her of the coming prophecy. The disruption of the witch's hold on her allows her to escape and she goes to StoneHaven. Once there, she projects herself into Calli's life and sets this entire adventure in motion."

I nod. "It's the only answer. There's no other way this could've worked out."

Lukas sets his glass down and whistles. "That explains how the Pixie Queen and Rowan knew to redirect the river in Pennsylvania too. We never could figure out how they did that a decade before we needed to safeguard a site for the portal gate."

Hawk nods. "Honor must've communicated it to them somehow and they started to divert the flow to shift the perception of where the sealed rift was located."

Calli shifts to the front of her seat and frowns. "Then the only question is where's Honor and how do we get her back?"

CHAPTER TEN

Rhylan

I'm torn. I see the Wolf King and Creed talking about Honor and making plans for the future and I know deep in the twist of my bowels they are a better choice for this realm's leadership, but to support them means to go against my brother, my mother, and our standing as one of the ancient dragon families.

The Silverwing name is in tatters since our father's challenge of Shadowcaster. It wouldn't survive defection to overthrow the crown.

I'm bound to Laryssa by duty.

I'm bound to Creed by desire.

I tip back the third bottle of ale I've opened in the last twenty minutes and let the oaky stout soothe some of my jagged edges.

"Why do you look like someone kicked you in the gem pouch?" Vikarus asks, walking through the open door to my suite. With the door to the corridor propped open, I can sit at my kitchen table and have a clear sightline of the door to the private suite of the royal heirs.

"Because I genuinely think we're on the losing side and I can't figure out how to stay on top of things and still keep ourselves and our name in good standing."

Vik opens my small countertop refrigerator and helps himself, pulling out a carton of raw meat. After ripping open the package of shaved venison, he sniffs it and decides it passes the test. "The reason you can't figure out how to flip allegiance and stay in good standing is because there isn't a way. We were given a task, first by Shadowcaster, and then by the queen of our realm. It's as simple as that."

I finish the ale in front of me and twist the top of the next bottle in line. "It's *not* as simple as that."

"Why not? You're not getting soft on me, are you?"

"Not soft—smart. We've got to think beyond our next move to what happens three moves after that."

Vik slumps down in the seat opposite me and snatches a bottle of ale out of the carton of eight. "That is your problem. You think too much. What you need to do is turn off your brain for a night and relax."

I lift the bottle in my hand and clink the mouth along the three bottles I've already emptied. The high-pitched *chink, chink, chink* of glass on glass rings in the air. "Here I am... relaxing."

Vik grins. "You can do better. Come on in, ladies."

My heart sinks as three of Vik's regulars round the door-frame and join us. One's a trylle, one's a water nymph, and one's a light faery. They're dressed for sex with tight sheath dresses that are so short, I can see the color of their underpants. And, what do you know, they are hemorrhaging the pheromones of girls who have needs to be filled.

I take a long draw on my drink and sigh. "I hate to disappoint you, ladies, but tonight's not your night for the dragon twins. Vik will have to tackle the delights himself, I'm afraid."

Vik makes a face at me. "What? Why would you turn down dragon doubles? You love it when we share."

I did... when we were adolescents. "Bad idea, my brother. I'm on duty."

He chuffs. "Since when has being on duty stopped us. Leave the door open. You'll see if anything happens that you need to take care of."

The idea that Creed or one of the others might come out and see me in the throes of release with these women turns my stomach. I never intended to claim him in front of them but if I join Vik with these women, it would be an intentional insult and dismissal of what happened.

My dragon claimed a mate.

And like it or not, somewhere deep, deep inside the man, I didn't object. Being with these women feels like a betrayal. Except, Creed's been having sex with the wolf and the bear and I have no say in that.

That was before my dragon staked his claim.

Now that I'm in the mix, I'm not sure what we're supposed to do. Will he have me in his life? The universe chose the wolf for him. What does that mean?

Blast, I'm confused.

The water nymph, Brook, doesn't wait for me to clear my mental cobwebs. She pulls the table forward and kneels in front of my chair. With a hand on each of my knees, she opens my legs and reaches for the buckle of my fatigues. "Vik's right. You are tightly strung. Aura, Ruby, and I can help you with that."

She releases the pin in the buckle holding my pants together and makes short work of opening things up. I bang my ale down and grip her wrists as foam rises up the neck and onto the table. "I appreciate the intention, but I can't. Prince Creed has a suite full of guests and I'm on duty. It's not a good night."

I push my chair back, but Brook has a hold of my cock and is not taking no for an answer. She crawls forward, trying to get over me and suck me into her mouth. "Slecking hell, you need to stop."

My pants are open, and I curse, pushing back in my chair, trying to gain some distance. "I said no."

The knock on the door breaks her determination.

Rolling out of her grasp, I stand, turn my back, and get things put away. Of all the slecking people...

I do up my pants and turn to the door. "Princess."

Keyla stands in the doorway taking in the scene. Unlike the three women in my suite, her gaze is sharp and intelligent. She's reading the room and knowing her sense of smell is more discerning than mine means she smells the wanton female hunger in the air.

I scrub a rough hand over my face and draw a steadying breath. "Apologies. What can I do for you?"

She smiles at the ladies. "May I ask your guests to excuse themselves so I can speak with you privately?"

"Of course, Princess," I say, thankful for at least that much. Throwing Vik a glare I point to the hall. "Like I said. Not a good night, my brother."

Vik frowns but isn't about to argue with the newly wedded princess of our realm in front of the girls. As far as the palace staff and civilian population know, we're Creed's bodyguards. Now that he's mated, that duty would extend to Keyla as well.

When my twin and his three companions clear out, I gesture for her to come in and check the hall to ensure we won't be overheard. "That wasn't what it looked like. I'd appreciate you not making an issue about it with Creed. I had no intention of starting something up with Vik and those women. I need you to believe me."

"All right," she says.

I wait, but when nothing more comes at me, I press on. "All right what? All right, you won't bring it up with Creed or that you believe me."

She shrugs. "Both. I overheard enough to know you were trying to diffuse your brother's plans and smelled enough to believe you were frustrated and trying to end the aggression to have your cock swallowed by that blue-skinned girl."

Classy. I grunt. "You don't mince words, do you?"

"Who has the time? Besides, there are more pressing matters to discuss."

"Yeah? Like what?"

"Like expectations of mating, loyalty, honor, duty... so many things. I'm a wildling, so I understand losing control, but I also understand what it means. You told Creed the two of you will ignore what happened, but at some point soon, your dragon will tire of knowing you're the odd man out. When that happens, you'll be a danger to everyone. We need to sort out your situation and get things resolved before that happens."

I lean back and check that the corridor is still clear. "You say whatever is on your mind, don't you?"

"Of course. There are times for discretion and diplomacy, but right now, the happiness of my mates, Honor's safety, and setting things right in this quadrant take precedence—in that order."

"And what, you're here because he's asking for me? I find that hard to believe."

She offers me a sad smile. "No. He's much too annoyed to be pining for you at the moment. *You* are the mate I was referring to. Your happiness is what I'm most worried about tonight."

I search her gaze for any hint that she's lying. Her words carry the warm, enticing scent of compassion and as much as I know scents don't lie, I'm not sure what to do with that. "I don't understand you. You've won. The universe gave him to you. Why do you care what happens to me?"

She shrugs. "Creed cares for you. We've been matched as mirrored souls, so I have to believe you're worth caring for. I didn't understand what you said this afternoon about your alpha, your mother, and your family name, but the panic and regret of your scent singed my nostrils. You think you're alone. You're not... or at least, you don't have to be."

"There's nothing you can do to help. There's nothing anyone can do. Even discussing it is dangerous. Just believe me when I say, you and Creed will be the death of my family."

"I won't let that happen."

"You won't have any choice."

Stepping close, she presses her hands flat on the muscled plains of my chest, raises onto her toes, and leans close to whisper in my ear. "I understand you neither like me nor trust me, but we're connected now."

The warmth of her hands bleeds through my shirt and I close my eyes.

"Tell us what you're up against, Rhy. We can work toward an outcome that works for all four of us. We don't have to be adversaries."

Her scent has altered since the searing. She and Creed have mated and their natural scents have merged. It calls my dragon to the fore in a rush.

Creed is ours. What is his, is ours too.

Unbidden, my body responds and my cock hardens. This close, there's no way she'll miss the hunger. Slecking hell, could this get any more twisted?

Her wolf lets off a low growl and my dragon responds in turn. The merging of sounds is rough and full of probing possibilities. Warm breath tickles the side of my neck as her touch seeps through the fabric of my shirt. Unlike the wanton aggression the other three women were oozing into the air, Creed's Little Wolf isn't after sex. She wants more than that.

More than I can give.

"Return to your suite, Princess. Your mates will be missing you soon."

She nuzzles her nose against the side of my neck, and I

freeze. Every survival instinct I possess rears and I have a violent urge to shove her away.

But I don't.

If she tenses to bare her teeth, I have enough strength to throw her across the suite like a ragdoll. Except she doesn't. She draws her tongue along the sensitive flesh of my throat and breathes me deep into her lungs. Her animal is taking stock of mine.

Her wolf lets off a soft growl of approval and my cock twitches behind the fastenings of my pants.

"You think you're his, but you belong to all of us now, Dragon. You're mine, Rhylan Silverwing, and I protect what's mine."

~

Keyla

I see the shock on Rhylan's face and smell the skepticism in the air. It's nothing less than I expect. I ease back and offer him a sultry grin. "Once you learn to trust us, you'll see the obstacles you're envisioning aren't as bad as you think."

"No offense, Princess, but you don't know shit about my problems."

I shift toward the table and let my hand brush across the front of his pants as I step away. He's hard and my wolf stretches languidly within. He wasn't ready for his dragon to claim Creed but there's no reversal of a wildling bond. He's bound to us.

So, if the man is too stubborn to come to his senses, I'll seduce his dragon and gain his trust that way. "Eventually, you'll need to let us in. The sooner you do that, the better."

"Better for who? Not me or Vik. Not my family."

I pick up the open bottle of stout on the table and bring it to my lips. Letting a couple of long swallows slide down my throat, I lick my lips. "Who would you rather have at your back, Creed, Doc, and me with the support of the Phoenix and her Guardians or a queen you don't believe in?"

"You don't understand."

"Then tell me." I set the beer down and stride back to meet him chest to chest. With a slow, gentle hand, I sweep the fall of his hair out of his eyes so I can read him better. "I guarantee I understand realm politics and the pressures of family reputation much better than you think. I'm more than the fated mate of your lover. I'm the Prime Princess of the Human Realm."

His gaze narrows and instead of appealing to the man, I return my attention to his dragon. There are certain things predatory males of wildling species can't ignore. Strength. Weakness. Challenge. And submission.

Standing so close, the heat of his body is raising the hair on my arms, I sweep my hair to one side and bring it forward. Giving him my back, I tilt my head and bare my neck to him.

The growl of his dragon is too quiet to be heard by human ears, but my wolf picks it up. It's a sorrowful bale and my heart goes out to him.

He's so torn and twisted up.

"We are mates, Rhylan Silverwing. If you would welcome it, I would ease you."

He chuffs. "Not interested."

Glancing over my shoulder, I smile, reading the lie in those words. "Tonight, when you're lying alone in bed and your mind won't stop spinning, I want you to reach between your legs and grip that hard length of steel trying to break free from your pants."

I turn and drop my gaze to where the black fabric of his military pants is straining to hold him. "Think about Creed and how badly your dragon needs to consummate its claim. Think about me naked in the suite today and what it would feel like to be inside me with Creed slamming hard into you from behind and my nails gripping your shoulders to ride out the storm. Think about belonging to something eternal where you'll be accepted and cherished for who you are."

A roar of dark spice fills the air. There's no way either of us could miss his mating scent and he knows I've won. He wants what I'm offering, he just needs to get out of his own way to make it happen.

"You need to leave, Princess," he says, his voice graveled with his dragon's ascension.

"You belong in there with us, Rhy. Let me help you get there."

I read the anguish in his eyes and my heart aches for him. Still, it's not time to push. He needs to decide he wants what's waiting for him across the hall... and not only the benefit of the mating.

I meant what I said, with the quint working with us, he has a greater chance of reaching his end goals on team Thornebane.

Leaving him to think about that, I head back and rejoin the party. The music bombards me the moment I open the door and I laugh at Jaxx, Doc, and Brant dancing with Calli in the center of the living room rug.

Creed is leaning against the wall inside the door and straightens when I come in. "How did it go with Rhy? He wasn't rude to you, was he?"

"Not at all."

Creed arches a brow looking skeptical.

"Seriously. We talked. Well, mostly I talked, and he listened. Then, once I said what I needed to, I left him to think about things. Nothing happened."

"I'm calling bullshit on that," Doc says, joining us. His cheeks are flushed and he's a little breathless. I love that the bears love to dance. He breathes deep and arches an ebony brow. "If you were just talking, why are you wearing his mating scent?"

Creed stiffens and I shake my head. "Seriously, nothing happened. As you said, the mind is a powerful sexual organ. His door was open the entire time."

"And?" There's no heat in Doc's expression, but I get the sense there's no way he's letting this go.

"All right, I may have had a rather suggestive subtext conversation with his dragon. We need to forge a relationship with his wild side or there will be trouble."

"What do you mean?" Creed asks. "You're talking like you think he's dangerous."

Doc nods. "Oh, he is... maybe not yet, but he will be. A mated wildling needs his mate. The more powerful the species, the more dangerous that need will become."

Creed frowns and looks at me. "What did you do?"

"Nothing. I merely coaxed his dragon forward a little with some female persuasion. Basically, I flirted with his animal to start winning over the man."

"And will that be enough?"

Doc and I both shake our heads. "I don't think so. Rhylan is stubborn. You might have to take one for the team and tame your dragon."

Doc chuckles and pats Creed's shoulder. "That's tomorrow's problem. What else did you talk about?"

I shrug. "I merely pointed out that even without the mating, having us at his back holds more potential for him to come out of things in one piece."

Creed grunts. "Laryssa certainly doesn't care about him. He knows that."

"And with the power of Kotah and the Phoenix Quint behind us, he belongs on team Thornebane."

"What did he say to that?" There's no missing the concern in Creed's gaze. He might be furious about the claiming and embarrassed about his salacious relationship with his prison guard, but the fact is, he cares about Rhylan and that goes both ways.

"We'll let him sleep on it," I say, the music making me sway. "But for tonight, I've got some dancing to catch up on. Do you want to cut a rug with me?"

Creed frowns and looks at his area rug.

Doc barks a laugh. "Human expression. Cut a rug means dance. There will be no assault on your décor."

My prince looks relieved. "Oh, no, you go have fun. I'm not a dancing prince."

I roll my eyes. "Yeah, you and Kotah both. Okay, have fun holding up the wall."

CHAPTER ELEVEN

Rhylan

*A*fter a miserable attempt at sleep, I give up and decide to start my day with a couple of bottles of ale and a hot shower. I strip naked, swallow down half of the first bottle, and pick up a second bottle to go. Not the most productive morning routine, but I'm past caring.

It's taking all I have to guard the prince and his lovers, lie to my brother, and pretend the evil bitch who holds my leash isn't waving the key to my destruction in front of my face.

What does it matter if I show up to work in the haze of inebriation? At least locking myself in and getting shit-faced keeps my dragon at bay.

As much as I hate it, Keyla wasn't wrong when she said my dragon won't be held off long. Claiming Creed was only a bandage on a hemorrhaging wound. The bleeding hasn't stopped.

He's sharing himself with two other lovers.

Pretending it doesn't gut me to be left across the hall while he's in the royal suite with them is necessary, but it doesn't fix anything.

I suck back another couple of gulps and reach into the shower to warm the water. With my thumb over the mouth of the bottle, I step under the spray.

I hiss and turn down the heat, my ass now screaming from the shock of being scalded.

Pressing the rim of the bottle to my lips, I finish bottle number one and set it down. I need to work on tightening up my emotions and locking down my dragon.

What an idiot I am.

For the briefest moment last night, I actually bought into the happily ever after bullshit Keyla dangled in front of my face.

Mates. The four of us against the world. Good conquering evil. Belonging to something to be proud of.

I see the bonds of camaraderie they share and yeah, I want that. She says it's as simple as confiding in them, but she hasn't got a clue. If she knew all of it... how far back Laryssa's meddling went... how she plotted with the avian's father... how they eliminated her father... she'd never accept me.

Slecking hell.

Tipping my head back under the stream of water, I close my eyes and let the sluice of hot and steamy run through my hair, down my back, and over my ass.

Mated.

My dragon's tantrum has really slecking screwed me over. I had feelings for Creed before, sure. I respected his strength, sympathized with his situation, and yeah, physically, there's no getting away from the obvious—the guy is ripped and sexy as a god.

But before the soul-searing, I was never conflicted like this. And I certainly wasn't homicidally dominant to take what is mine.

Reaching under the dispenser, I wait for a puddle of soap to drop into my palm and then start moving it over my pecs. Once I get my froth on, I let those slick hands do their thing.

My mind flips back to Keyla's visit last night.

The look in those warm, brown eyes, as she told me things could be different. The altered scent of her skin when she exposed her neck to me. The feel of her tongue on my throat as she tasted my flesh and her wolf called me home.

Unbidden, my dragon stretches within me, luxuriating in the heat of that moment.

Sure, she'd been baiting me, seducing me toward switching sides, but intentions aside, she offered me exactly what I want.

My dark and twisted prince.

Whether I regret it or not, Creed responded to my dragon's claim. Pinned against that wall, he wanted what I offered. Every moan and thrust and scent at that moment is etched into my memory.

He submitted—which surprised me, given how aggressive he's always been when we're together—but once our bodies were locked and I claimed his vein, he gave me the power.

I groan as my cock surges. The magic of his blood still rushes through my veins like a drug. And after only one taste, I am addicted.

I take my time shampooing, and let those memories mingle with the reality of who we are.

Enemies with benefits.

Sweeping my palm down the sculpted ridges of my torso, a moan rumbles from my chest when I grab hold of my cock. My erection kicks in my hand and I draw a deep breath. Is this what I've been reduced to? Jacking off in the shower to my self-destructive mistakes?

I rinse the suds off my hands and bend to grab the next bottle of ale from the floor outside my shower. If I'm going to do this, I might as well do it right.

The next few gulps of ale go down easy, and I lower the

trajectory of the nozzles and turn on the buffing cloths. Closing my eyes, I let the dark stout flow over my tongue, crank up the rotation speeds, and let things take their course.

Shit that feels good.

I play back the sensations of claiming him: Creed's blood flowing down my throat and feeding my hunger, the rise and fall of his mighty chest pumping against mine, the solid shaft of his cock in my grip as I palmed him rough.

Leaning back against the cold tile, I take hold of my cock and settle into a rhythm.

I swallow another gulp of ale and miss the tastes of my dark-souled prince... his blood, his sweat, and best of all, his cum. Shit, I love to suck him off.

I set the bottle on the ledge opposite me and brace myself against the shower wall. Leaning forward, I watch the crown of my cock pop free from my palm and then get swallowed with each rapid stroke. The pressure building in my balls is so agonizingly good.

The scent of his skin...

I close my eyes and breathe deep. Slecking hell, it's like he's —my eyes flip wide and I curse.

It's not me imagining his scent.

Creed *is* here and he's naked.

When he steps into the shower it strikes me there are a dozen things I should do to diffuse this. I need to protest. I need to send him back to his mates. I need to draw a line for both our sakes.

I don't do any of them.

This is a terrible idea.

He's in my space. Vik could walk in. And even if he doesn't come until after, Creed's scent will be in here. The man has two mates waiting for him across the hall why does he have to be here screwing up my life?

I need to object.

I need to stop this.

I need to talk to him.

No. No talking. Talking will ruin everything and rob me of this moment.

Lifting my chin, I grip both sides of Creed's chiseled jaw and pull his mouth to mine. When those velvet lips meet mine, I kiss him with all the desperation I've been pushing down for the past week.

My need is an over-inflated beach ball shoved underwater. The moment our bodies connect, all that pent-up rejection releases, shooting out of the water in a dizzying fury.

The two of us are grasping, crashing together in abandon. Lips, tongues, and hands, all frantic.

And it's not only me who's desperate. When Creed pulls back to suck in a breath, his eyes are wild, his expression tormented. "I'm still furious with you."

"Understood."

"I fucking hate how it went down."

"Agreed."

He drops to his knees and takes me into his mouth.

He's not gentle and I have to pike at the waist and catch my weight on the opposite wall to accommodate his seizure of my cock. I curse and my dragon ascends in a rush.

Slecking hell, he pushes my control.

Watching his head bob and twist over my cock is too much. His silver hair is wet and I slick my hand over the back of his head to keep him in place.

My release was already close when he arrived, there's no holding it back.

I grunt, panting as I grip his hair and spill into his greedy mouth.

The shout of my release echoes off the hard surfaces and

bounces back at us from all angles. My body goes rigid, convulsing in a series of mind-shattering spasms that run the length of my spine.

As the chaos of the last few moments ebbs out of me, the room begins to swim. Maybe it's the power of the release or the steamy heat of the shower or the emotion swimming in my head... who cares.

Before I go down, Creed's got his arms around me and shuts off the water. A moment later, I'm on my stomach on the bathroom floor.

The tiny bathmat doesn't save much of my skin from the icy chill of being lain out on the tile. Still, the cool does wonders for clearing my head. I take a few cleansing breaths and realize Creed isn't finished with me yet.

The shiver that runs the length of my spine has more to do with the anticipation of what's to come than the icy granite tiles I'm lying on.

Dripping wet, Creed crawls up my back, his erection brushing the inside of my thighs like something in an erotic dream.

"I'm still furious with you," he says again, lowering himself between my legs.

That's fine. He can be furious with me.

Hell, *I'm* furious with me.

I glance back, lock gazes with him, and nod. Whatever he needs to do to ease my betrayal I'll do. He has my consent. He can take me hard and use me if that's what works. I'm just so glad to be part of the process.

"I need inside you."

That's good because I was thinking the same thing. "There's liquid in that drawer."

The soft hiss of my vanity drawer opening is followed by the *pop* of the tilting seal of a lubrication bottle. Honestly, I'm surprised he's opting for the lube. When he's really angry, he punishes us both by leaving things raw.

I don't care how raw we get. He's holding all the power right now and we both know it.

"On your knees."

I push up and dry my palms on the mat so I can brace my weight against the floor and ready for what comes next.

Creed slicks lubricant on me and mounts me from behind. My spent arousal pulses with a reawakening. The invasion is fast, the fullness of him thrusting deep very welcome. Angry or not, the stinging pleasure of being taken by my mate makes my wild side roar.

"This is for your dragon," he says, pushing deep and then receding. "Keyla and Doc are worried about your animal side and the safety of those around you."

I clench my jaw, Creed's rhythm quickly growing to be fast and furious. "They know you're here?"

"Of course," he grunts. "They are my mates. I will never betray them."

I'm not sure what I think about that...

Actually, I do. It's a huge hit to my ego. Somewhere inside me, I envisioned Creed sneaking over to be with me because they weren't enough, that he couldn't get what he needed from them and secretly craved me.

That's not the case.

Still, he's here with me now and that's something—no, it's everything. Pushing all thoughts of the rest of it away, I focus on the pleasure of being with Creed. The grip of his fingers on my hips. The demanding rhythm of his thrusts. The breathy sounds he makes when he's getting close to detonating and marking my insides.

No matter how many times we do this, I always end up needing him more.

My balls tighten as I head toward another release. His scent is everywhere, and I'm lost in it. His scent has altered since the last time we were together. Last night, I smelled Creed in Keyla's scent, now I smell her in his.

Despite what she told me to do, I *didn't* picture her naked for a rub and tug in the wee hours. Maybe I should have. Maybe then I could've gotten some sleep.

While having her scent singeing my nostrils at this moment there's no helping it.

I call up the image of her naked in the living room yesterday. I remember the soft curves of her hips and the lush heaviness of her breasts.

"We are mates, Rhylan Silverwing. If you would welcome it, I would ease you."

~

Creed

I sense the moment Rhylan's mind shifts and curse. He's close. I know he is. Keyla and Doc explained how dangerous unacknowledged wildling mates can get—and he's a dragon. For his sake and ours, he needs to remain stable. I don't want him to lose this release.

Opening a mental channel, I...

"We are mates, Rhylan Silverwing. If you would welcome it, I would ease you."

My rhythm falters for a moment as I see Keyla in his mind. She's naked and he's very curious about her.

If you're curious, let me show you what it's like to be mated to her.

Before he can argue, I open the library of my recent memories. I show him sensual clips of Keyla on her knees and the glory of how tightly her pussy squeezes my cock when I'm inside her.

I let him feel the suction of her hot little mouth as she toys with my crown and swallows my cum. I share the throaty, feminine sounds she makes as Dillan and I wind her up and the growl of her wolf when she's pitching over the edge of her control.

Rhylan's release hits hard and I reach around his hip to grip his cock. Hips locked forward, shoulders rigid, head back, he's exquisite as he spills over my hand.

Stroking him off, I ride out his release, remembering every sensual, seductive detail of what it is to be naked with her. Then, as his breathing settles, I play him back the non-sexual moments.

The sound of her laughter when she's fooling around on the dancefloor with Jaxx. The playful grin she flashes me when she's teasing me about something. The tenderness in her gaze when she looks at our bear and doesn't realize I'm watching.

"You love her," Rhy says, easing forward and shifting to face me. "I thought it was just the searing."

I draw a deep breath and stand. "It's not the searing. I don't know if it's love yet, but it's well on its way to becoming that."

"Wait," he says, frowning at the robe in my hand. "You didn't finish."

I wave that away. "Like I told you. This was for your dragon, not me."

His golden brows come down hard as he launches to his feet. "What? So, that meant nothing? I don't want your slecking pity, Creed. Screw you."

Before I can argue, his right cross snaps my head back as blood bursts from my nose. I stagger over to the sink and run the cold water, grabbing a cloth. "Fucking, hot-headed dragon."

"You deserved that," he growls. "How dare you come in here if it didn't mean anything to you. That's low. That's really slecking low."

I rinse the blood from my face, get into my robe, and press the cold cloth over my nose. "No, you idiot. What's low is sucker-punching your mate before he has a chance to answer your fucking question. Dammit. You're such a jerk."

"So, it did mean something? Shit, Creed. I'm sorry."

I roll my eyes and head for the door. "You're an emotional yo-yo, dragon. Get a fucking grip or you're going to get us all killed."

CHAPTER TWELVE

Doc

The door to Rhylan's suite opens and Creed exits in a rush. "How'd that go—oh, shit." I scowl at the blood staining his face and hands and usher him across the hall, straight through the suite, and into the bathroom.

Keyla's still sleeping, so we're quiet as we pass through the bedroom and close the door.

Grabbing a facecloth, I run it under the faucet and set to work doctoring my mate. "So, I take it, he didn't welcome your advances?"

Creed grunts. "The sex went fine. He was mad when I got up to leave. He didn't like the fact that I was there to level out his dragon and not for some heart-felt mating moment."

There's so much anger in Creed's scent I can't tell if that's because he's been clocked in the face, because of the mating, or because Rhylan got it wrong and maybe there was heart-felt mating in their moment and the dragon missed it.

"It's broken and you're going to have one helluva black eye."

"Fuck me. I can't go around looking like I'm a royal

punching bag. Laryssa will investigate how it happened and then Rhylan will be in more trouble than he is already."

I chuckle. "You're worried about him, so I take it you haven't given up on him."

The annoyance in his gaze tugs at my heart. "I wish I could. Life would've been much easier if there wasn't something between us. I tried to quit him more than once. He just has this way of getting under my skin."

"Hey, no judgment. You love who you love." I rinse the cloth and the water runs pink in the basin of the sink. "I'm a great doctor, but even I can't erase this mess, so it never happened. Calli can, though."

Drying my hands on my jeans, I reach under the counter and grab the bag I packed when I came here three days ago. Unzipping the side pocket, I pull out a small, glass vial. "We all carry phoenix tears now in case we're separated and hurt. A few drops will fix you up."

I sit him on the edge of the jet tub and unscrew the cap of the vial. Calli's tears look like water but in direct light, they sparkle with the healing magic they hold.

Creed closes his eyes while I cover the area and spread the moisture with my finger. "I'm sorry, Bear. It seems a shame to waste such a powerful cure-all on a broken nose."

"Yeah, well, like you said. It doesn't do us any good if our hot-headed dragon mate gets called into the principal's office."

I finish administering the tears, zip the vial back into my bag, and go back to the sink. "Not to be indelicate, but the sexing went okay? His dragon is appeased?"

"His dragon is fine. The man is the problem."

I chuckle. "Yeah, we wildlings can be stubborn and a little broody."

Creed rolls his eyes and winces. "And I'm mated to three of you."

I grin and point to the shower. "You smell like dragon sex.

Clean up and I'll check in with Hawk. Maybe he and Lukas have a plan on how to find your sister and the blood witch."

"Thanks, Bear."

I hold up my fist and he bumps my knuckles. "I got you. I mean that. We're in this for the long haul."

Leaving our prince to pull himself together, I head out of the suite and into the corridor. Drawing a deep breath, I curse at the lingering scent of a Creed and Rhylan hook up in the air.

If it's out here... changing course, I knock on Rhylan's door as I let myself in.

The dragon looks up from where he's kicked back on his bed with a bottle of booze. His hair is wet and brushed back over his head. With a clear view of his face and eyes, I'm stunned.

The guy could pass as a Norse god. And, hello, he's a piercing boy.

He's also hitting the liquid sedation hard. "Fuck, dragon. Now is not the time."

He tilts his head to the side and scowls at the door. "I'm not sure how things are done in your realm, Bear, but in the Fae Realm, a closed door means something."

"I came because the corridor still holds an ode to your sexcapade and I wanted to check out things in here. Which is much worse, by the way."

He shrugs. "What does it matter? I'm ruined ten different ways. I might as well accept it."

My bear lets off a long rumble. "Your tenacity is underwhelming."

I follow the scent of sex and smile as it leads me into the bathroom. Awesome. If they'd been in the main room on the bed, I'd have the air and sheets and a dozen other things to deal with.

Score!

Flicking on the switch for the fan, I start clearing the air. I lift my nose and draw a deep breath.

The cum spilled out on the floor mat is the biggest problem. Scooping that up, I take it to the sink and open the faucet.

"Doctor, soldier, and you moonlight as a chambermaid," Rhylan says, tipping back the bottle. "Triple threat."

I squeeze a glob of soap into the mat and meet his gaze in the mirror. "I've healed Creed's face and have him showering and cleaning up. Right now, you are the weakest link. Now, get your naked ass into that erotic carwash of a shower and get buffing."

His blond brow arches. "I'm alpha, you're beta. If we're mates, you need to get that hierarchy straight."

"I'm not sure how things are done in your realm, Dragon," I say, throwing his words back at him, "but in the Human Realm, beta doesn't mean I'm a weak pushover. It means I'm not driven with the aggression and testosterone to always be the asshole in charge. My strength and intelligence work just fine."

Pulling the plug on the sink drains the water and I wring out the mat. After hanging it over the inside of the tub, I draw another long pull of the air.

The ventilation system is doing wonders.

Striding up close and personal with our recent plus one, I take the bottle from his hands and tilt my head. "Shower. Pull your shit together. Nothing has changed. Sure, it's complicated but we've got your back, mate. The only way you've been screwed this morning is the good way. What happens next is on you."

When he curses and steps under the flow of water, I consider my work here done. There's a faint scent of blood in the main room, but that's better than sex. I'll take that as a win and take my leave.

Rhylan

Slecking bear. I'm not sure why he thinks he gets a say in any of this, but that doesn't seem to matter. I finish off in the shower, get dressed for duty, and eat a slice of bread, hoping it will soak up some of the alcohol sloshing around in my gut.

"Hey," Vik says, letting himself in.

"Is there a sign on my door that says, 'Don't knock, just come in? because holy hell, I need to start using the deadbolt."

Vik scowls. "I see a night's sleep hasn't improved your disposition any."

"Yeah, well, sleep is a luxury I was denied."

Vik's grin is annoying as hell. "So, that's why you turned down my female offerings. You had something scheduled already. Why didn't you just say so."

I give him my back and grab my weapons belt from the hook by the door. "Sorry to disappoint. I tossed and turned in my sheets all night and there was no one there to witness it."

"Well, then, I take it back. You need to get laid, my brother. You're coming unraveled."

"I'm painfully aware of that, thanks. Now, why are you here?"

"You asked me to give you a heads up on Laryssa's progress reconnecting with the other Whitehouse son."

I buckle the belt and check the charge of my sidearm. "And?"

"And she's headed to StoneHaven this morning to instruct the traveler she's using as a messenger."

"And you're joining her?"

"No. You are."

"Me? Why? You're her favorite lap dog."

"Yeah, well, she thinks you're slecking up with the prince. You let him go to Clarinta to meet with the royal liaison, you let him make that public announcement about the phoenix and the rift opening and you let him claim his mates. She's pissed."

I curse. "I didn't *let* him claim his mates. If it were up to me he wouldn't have anyone in his bed."

Vikarus hears the truth in my words and doesn't question why I feel so strongly. "I'm with you, but it changes nothing."

"So, now I'm stuck babysitting the queen?"

"Honestly, my brother, I think it's her who's babysitting you. And maybe it's less about babysitting and more about assessing your dedication to getting things done."

That bites my balls. "That's stupid. She wants control over Creed but she doesn't want us to alienate the Wolf King. Those two things are diametrically opposed."

He shrugs. "Stop making excuses. She's not wrong. You've been off your game and she doesn't even know about you letting him get away in the Human Realm. You never did explain how that happened."

I rub a hand over my mouth. I'm not about to tell Vik that Creed has his powers back. The only chance he has of righting the atrocities of Laryssa's reign is for him to be able to defend himself.

So, if it all has to fall at my feet, so be it. "Fine. You keep the prince in line and I'll go with the queen to StoneHaven. Creed and his mates are escorting the Wolf King and his mates to Rames and Travon to make first contact and start talks regarding the portal coordinates."

"Or so they think," Vik says. "Not on my watch. I'm the slecking dragon guard of the Queen of Dornte. They're looking at a non-eventful day in the castle."

I chuff. "Well, obviously you haven't been paying attention. It's fine though. I'll leave you to handle them your own way. Good luck."

"Luck is for suckers," Vik says. "I've got skills."

I nod. "You sure do. You're one talented asshole."

Keyla

I wake with a low-grade hangover and the sun of mid-morning burning warm and bright through the leaded windows of Creed's bedroom. Shielding my gaze, I roll the other direction and find Doc relaxing next to me. He's propped up on a mound of pillows with one arm behind his head and the other holding an open book.

"Good morning. What are you reading?"

He tilts it to show me the cover. "A historical text about the powerful families behind the wars and how they ended up when the chips fell."

As interesting as that sounds, the pain behind my eyes prohibits me from being excited about reading in any way. Shifting under the sheets, I scoot closer and lay my cheek on his chest.

I close my eyes as he strokes my hair and wonder if this realm has headache tablets.

I must've dozed off because the next time I open my eyes, there is a hiss of running water coming from the bathroom and Creed is crossing the room with a towel wrapped around his hips and another draped over his shoulders to catch the water from his hair.

"Good morning," I say, rolling onto my belly to watch his powerful stride.

"Good afternoon, Little Wolf." He chuckles and changes course to meet me for a kiss.

"Did you pay a visit to our surly dragon this morning as we discussed?"

"I did. The dragon is sated. The man is a jerk."

The tone of his voice is so laced with emotion, I decide to leave that one alone for now. "You sound like you could use a little TLC."

He shakes his head. "And what might that mean, my minxy mate?"

I grip the tucked knot of his towel and pull the fabric free. "Let me show you."

Not waiting for an answer, I reach around his hips and pull him forward until his crotch is tight to the edge of the mattress. Creed groans as I place his soft cock into my mouth and suckle and play until his solid erection kicks against my tongue.

"Fiery hell, you're a quick study."

I suck to the end and pop off like a kid devouring a lollipop. "I'm an eager student. So, TLC. It stands for tender loving care. Feeling a bit better?"

"Much, thank you. That was lovely."

I laugh. "Oh, I'm not done. I was simply pausing to check if you have the time for me to devour you."

He chuckles. "I think any male given the choice would make time to have his very sexy, very sweet mate suck on him."

"Good answer, my prince." I drop my head and get back to business. Wriggling on top of the bed, I get into a comfortable position and settle in to take my time.

Creed's body being hairless is so strangely erotic it's crazy. As I nuzzle and nip, my wolf lets off a low, steady growl of approval. Part of having an animal side is understanding that our animals like to play. I'm not sure if humans are the same way, but wildlings love to let our playful sides out.

Creed doesn't seem to mind.

I take my time, pleasuring him, while at the same time taking pleasure myself. He places a gentle hand on the back of my head and curses as his hips start a slow and steady rock into my mouth.

I smile inwardly and reach beneath his shaft to the heavily weighted sac swaying free. Probing, I massage the delicate orbs within.

"Oh, Princess," he whispers. "You shatter me."

Moist heat trickles against the sensitive folds of my core and my wolf lets off a growl.

"That sound..." he growls. "You have no idea what that does to me. Growl for me again, Little Wolf."

I growl again, but this time it's hot and hungry.

His fingers tighten in my hair and his breathing catches. "I'm going to come. If you don't want me in your mouth, now is your chance to—"

I grip his balls tighter and lock in. There's no way I'm giving this up.

His body bows forward over me and his palms plant on the mattress on either side of my ribs. The rest of his sentence is lost within a throaty shout.

Warm spurts of cum cream my tongue and I swallow his release. Unlike the saltiness of Doc's seed, Creed's is sweet with a little tingle of magic against my tongue. Wanting all he can give, I suck and swallow, riding out every wave of his orgasm.

"Your mouth is so hot and sweet."

"So, is your cum. I want more."

He barks a laugh. "Always hungry for more, aren't you? Is that because of the newness of us specifically or the newness of sex in general?"

"I have no idea. I only know I can't help it."

"I don't want you to help it." He rolls me onto my back and points toward the pillow. "I do want to return the favor though."

I swivel across the covers and bite my lip. "You don't have to. That was all for you."

Creed chuckles. "It's only fair that I get to torture you a little after you ambushed me and sucked me dry."

I stretch back and let my knees fall open. "Well, all right. Fair is fair, I suppose."

CHAPTER THIRTEEN

Doc

I wait for the ride to come to a full and complete stop before exiting the shower. Those twirling buffing cloths in conjunction with the pivoting spray nozzles leave me feeling clean and yet dirty at the same time.

Toweling off, I open the bathroom door to let out some of the steam. The moment the fresh air of the bedroom hits me, I'm smacked with the wafting wonder of Keyla's feminine scent.

Well, well, what have we here?

Keyla's arousal wraps around me. It squeezes my insides and brings my bear roaring forward. When we first mated, I thought knowing Creed was touching her would drive us to violence.

It doesn't.

When the two of them are together, I see nothing but the beauty of their bodies twining, smell nothing but the rich scents of their hunger, and hear nothing but the throaty sounds of erotic perfection.

I thought seeing them together would make me feel like I

needed to have my turn, that I was being left out, that I should be up next.

If I adopted that mentality the three of us would never get out of this suite.

I take a seat in the chair opposite the bed and settle in to watch the show. The two of them don't seem to notice my arrival. And why would they?

They are busy... and getting busy.

Creed is draped over Keyla's lush body her long chestnut hair fanned out on the pillow. They're both naked and honestly, they are beautiful together. Creed's pale smooth skin next to the warm cinnamon complexion of Keyla's heritage is striking.

By the strength of sexual release in the air they have each already had one turn and now he's making love to her. Creed shoves his hand into the dark depths of Keyla's hair and his eyes roll closed.

He groans, kissing her more softly and with more affection than I've ever seen from him.

That's good. Until now, the only thing I've witnessed between the two of them is the wild and rough result of passions unhinged.

Keyla deserves soft sultry seduction as well.

Our girl is the picture of perfection, lying on that lush bed, so poised and proper and yet so incredibly sexual. There's a wildness in her that goes beyond her wolf.

Not wanting to disturb them, I open the flaps of the towel wrapped around my hips and take hold of the throbbing column between my thighs.

Brant asked last night who hadn't had a hand job in front of a room full of people. I'm not sure this counts but who the fuck cares.

Keyla undulates against Creed, stroking herself and at the same time stroking him. And since the two of them are having fun stroking, why shouldn't I?

I ease my ass down the seat a little to lean back and gain some extra room to move. My cock is granite hard and the glide and slide feels good after the tension of the morning. I tighten my grip and increase the pressure.

Watching them, especially with them not knowing I'm in the room, is a little dark and dirty.

It gets me off.

Everything is still so new. The three of us have had a few encounters but there is so much we haven't tried.

Creed's lips glide down her neck, his tongue stroking over her racing pulse. When he sucks on her skin, my erection kicks in my grip.

I feel her pleasure radiating through me.

I don't know if it's real or if Creed's emotional gift has taken root somehow but it's heady and powerful. Keyla whimpers, wrapping her legs around his hips. Digging her heels into his ass, she pulls him deeper.

My hand pumps my cock, and the soft *tic, tic, tic* of pre-cum marks the frenzied rhythm. My chest rises and falls with short, shallow breaths.

Creed lets off a grumbling moan, his sweet seduction discarded for some hard and hot fucking.

"Yes!" Keyla shouts, arching beneath him. "That's perfect... Don't stop..."

"Squeeze me, Little Wolf. Squeeze my dick."

Keyla throws her head back as a ragged sound tears from her throat.

"Yes, angel... just like that. Squeeze me just like—oh, fuck!"

Creed thrusts hard for a handful of frenzied strokes and then is overtaken by his release. The convulsive shudder racks his powerful frame, followed by an agonized sound of ecstasy. He pins his hips against Keyla's core erupting violently, flooding her with his heat.

There's no hope for me holding out.

I pump my cock once, twice more, and then I'm coming along with them, spurting hotly onto my abdomen and all over my hand.

I'm not sure if it's the breathy grunt of my orgasm or the scent of my release that catches Keyla's attention but as I spill, her gaze finds mine, the stunning brown of her eyes alight with sexual euphoria.

~

Creed

Well, that got away from me. When I rolled Keyla onto the bed, my intention was simply to return the gentle offering she had given me... but like everything else that's happened since Keyla came into my life things got out of control.

And like everything that has happened since Keyla came into my life that out-of-control chaos was worth it.

Pulling out of the warmth of her core is like being robbed every damn time. Maybe it's the magic of the searing but in those moments when I'm inside my mate there is nothing and no one that matters more to me.

She has quickly become my strength and my purpose. Rhylan said I'm in love with her, but it's too soon to put a label on it. All I know is the thought of losing her or living even a moment of life without her nearly brings me to my knees.

I must make my world safe for her.

A shift in the corner brings my attention to Dillan rising from one of the chairs in the reading nook. He's naked, semi-hard, and when he slips back into the bathroom to use the sink I have a fairly good idea what he was doing in that chair.

The thought of him watching us strikes me right in the stones. "I think our bear played the part of voyeur," I whisper against Keyla's shoulder.

"I don't think he was the only one."

I follow Keyla's gaze toward the open bedroom door and the living room beyond. Rhylan is standing in the next room, his dark gaze hooded, his muscled frame locked.

Rearing up on my knees, I twist towards the bathroom. "Your turn to get cleaned up, angel. Doc spoke with your brother this morning. Hawk and Lukas were going to check in with their team first thing. When you're ready we'll go across the hall and see what they came up with."

Keyla rolls to her feet and strides off to join our bear in the bathroom. I hop off the bed, grab the discarded towel from the floor, and wrap my hips.

"Since you haven't tried to retreat or punch me in the face, I take it you have something to say."

Rhy rubs a rough hand across his face and sighs. "I owe you a real apology. Yesterday my dragon took control, and I changed the course of your life and the lives of your mates. I was in shock and too wrapped up in my problems to realize it at the time. I truly am sorry to have taken your choice away from you."

"Thank you. I appreciate that."

"My second apology is for jumping to conclusions and lashing out at you this morning. Punching you was wrong. You were there for me with good intentions and didn't deserve my fist in your face."

I cross my arms over my chest. "And what brought on this epiphany of rational thinking?"

He tilts his head toward my bathroom and frowns. "Your wolf said something that rang true when she came to see me last night."

I hold up a finger. "You may call her Princess, Nakeyla, or Keyla. I don't even mind you referring to her as my wolf, but if you do, you need to take the snide tone out of your voice, or you'll get *my* fist to your face."

He frowns. "She's really under your skin, isn't she?"

"She's amazing, Rhy. Her bear is amazing. Her family is amazing. I don't know if it's because they were raised in the other realm, but they care about people—genuinely care—and are willing to step in and help."

The hopelessness in his expression hollows me out. "There's no helping me. My lot in life was set a decade ago. Vik and I are pawns, nothing more."

"What happened? Why does it have to be that way?"

"Because it *is* that way."

"Then explain it to me. Make me understand what keeps you loyal to her. Does she have someone you love prisoner? Is it a full-circle thing? I could understand that. You know what I've endured keeping Honor and my mother safe."

The agony in his gaze cleaves me in two.

"Sadly, some people are born a prince or a princess, and others aren't."

I have no idea what that means but I don't like the sound of it. "Your dragon changed that by claiming me. We're connected now... all of us."

He shakes his head. "That was a mistake—you and I both know that. The spell Lukas cast on us will keep our scents free from one another and no one who wasn't in that room will ever know. It's easier if I stay away and you focus on your new life."

Rhy moves to exit and suddenly I'm in his way.

I didn't realize I moved until I'm a solid wall between him and the door. "Rhy, don't. We might be a mess of a mating four-some, but they're great... and if you're worried about Keyla protesting, don't. She had already broached the subject of adding you in before you claimed me. They've been cool about all of it."

"That's my point," he says, his voice little more than a whis-per. "It's a mess because of me. You never invited me into your future, I inserted myself. Now, I'm righting that wrong."

In the silence that follows I feel like I should say something that makes this easier for him, better for all of us. I've got nothing.

"How do we pretend like it didn't happen? You're part of us now. To hide it will be a lie."

His lids close briefly, and he seems to steel himself. "Like you said before, lying is what I do, right? Vik's a dick and Rhy will lie."

I stiffen. "What makes... why would you say that?"

The pain that flashes in his eyes cuts me to the core. "It's something you said some nights when you fell asleep... after. I figure it's your psyche reminding you not to attach real feelings to what we did in the dark."

"Yeah, well, that failed miserably, didn't it?"

Rhylan points at the door behind me. "I said what I came to say. Vik's your guard today, so I'll see you when I see you."

The expression on Rhylan's face hollows me out. There's something in his voice too, but I don't know what I'm missing. When he steps past me, I grip his arm and pull him against my side. "What's going on? What aren't you saying?"

He shrugs. "Nothing worth worrying about. Take care, Creed. And make sure those mates of yours watch your back."

Why does it sound like he's saying goodbye?

"Vik's on duty, but we'll catch up later, right?"

"Sure, yeah, later. Look. I gotta go. Duty calls."

I suppose that's fitting.

He's always chosen his duty over everything else.

He leaves and the door latches with a soft click—not a slam, not a bang, just a quiet retreat. It strikes me that's telling of our relationship too.

The two of us are a whisper in the darkness.

A dirty secret.

"Hey... are you okay?" Doc asks.

A warm hand squeezes the flesh of my shoulder and I flinch. "I don't know. That was weird. He was acting really weird."

"Was he all right?"

"I don't think so."

A shiver runs my spine and I remember I have no shirt on and both he and Keyla are standing behind me.

They must see the scars.

They know I've been butchered.

I bite back the burn of acid climbing the back of my throat. "Sorry. I need to get dressed."

When I step into the closet, I close the wall and seal myself in. Suddenly, my mind is spinning, and I'm looking for something to use if I throw up.

With my back to the wall, I sink to the floor and put my head between my knees.

Is this about Rhylan denying his claim or him acting weird or my mates realizing I'm as damaged as I am?

I honestly don't know but my mind is fucked, and I need to pull myself together.

There's a knock on the wall and I close my eyes. Maybe if I don't answer, they'll go away.

"It's just me," Doc says, his voice low. "I sent Keyla across the hall to check on the quint. May I come in?"

"No. I'm hiding. You said I was entitled."

There's a soft male chuckle on the other side of the panel. "If you seriously don't want me to bother you, I'll go, but I'm here if you need someone to act as a sounding board."

I draw a deep breath and exhale. What was I saying to Rhy about them being amazing, caring people? It's not like I can get away with threesome sex and not have one of them see my back eventually. "Yeah, come in."

The panel swings open and the male steps in and closes things up again. "Hey, there."

"Hey, back."

"So, a tough moment all around."

I nod, becoming all too aware that I'm sitting on the floor of my closet wearing a towel. "I guess I really should get dressed."

Before I can get up, Doc squats down in front of me and meets my gaze. "Did you ever have to serve during the Wars of Power?"

I'm not sure why he's asking, but I don't really care. It's nice not to talk about why I'm curled up like a weakling among my dress wear. "No. The wars ended when I was a teenager and my father wouldn't have allowed it, even if they hadn't."

Doc nods. "Well, when I was younger, I was a handful. I ran with a rough crowd and got into trouble. Early on, my father gave up and I went into foster care. After getting arrested for the fifth time, my foster father, Ben, marched me down to the recruitment offices and signed me up for the military."

That doesn't sound like the man I know, but hey, I've only known him for four days. "I'm sorry."

He shakes his head. "It was the best thing that ever happened to me. I found myself in the armed forces, first as a soldier, then special ops, and briefly as an intelligence officer. The structure was good for me."

"I'm sure you were good at it."

He nods. "I excelled. I saw and did a lot of terrible things, but I was a soldier and had a purpose. I knew who I was and what I was there to do."

He looks off in the distance as if seeing the scene in his mind's eye. "One afternoon, my unit got caught in the wrong place at the wrong time. When the streets lit up with gunfire, I was injured. When I shipped home, I wasn't whole. It took a long time and a lot of love from my foster family to mold me back into the paragon of excellence you mated."

I chuckle. "It seems like you've got it all pulled together now."

He nods. "It took some doing but I got there. Can I show you something? It's the reason I'm telling you all this and I think it might help."

"Sure."

He stands to his full height, unbuttons his pants, and strips himself bare to his thighs. Sweeping his cock to the side, he points to his gem pouch. The skin is scarred and doesn't hang symmetrically and looks like his genitals have been mangled. "I caught a spray of bullets to the groin, lost one testicle, and got shipped home as damaged goods."

Having only been with the guy from behind, I hadn't noticed the scar, but yeah, it looks gnarly.

"Before I enlisted, and during my time as a soldier, I'd been promiscuous and very active. When I came home with this... well, I kinda froze myself out of the game by running toxic narratives in my head... I was brutalized, less of a male, no one would be able to stomach the sight of it or worse... they'd ask me about it. Any of this sounding familiar."

I sigh. "Word for word, actually. And here I thought I was the mind reader of the group."

He pulls his pants back up and puts things away. "My point is, whatever you've been through, it's in the past. I have no doubt it's a sore point and you'd rather stick a blade into your own stomach and gut yourself rather than talk about it, amirite?"

I dip my chin. "Pretty much."

"So, leave it at that for now. One day you'll want to get it off your chest and Keyla and I will hear you out. We'll talk about it, and the weight you bear because of what you suffered will ease a little. But do you know what we'll never do?"

"What's that?"

"Judge you for something that happened to you. It won't change who you are in our eyes. We won't pity you but we will empathize. It'll take time for it to sink way down deep into your marrow, but you are safe with us. Forever and always."

I'm not sure that's true. A fae without his wings is pathetic, but I appreciate the thought behind what he's saying. "Thanks, Bear. That helps, honestly."

Doc nods and holds out his hand to help me up. He's grinning and chuckles as I get to my feet.

"What's the look for?"

"That was my first mate pep talk and I nailed it."

I laugh and grab a shirt off the rack. "Yes, you did."

He winks and heads for the handle on the wall that opens things up to the bedroom. "All right, finish getting dressed and when you're ready, we'll head across the hall and find out what the plan is. We've got women to find and a queen to overthrow."

CHAPTER FOURTEEN

Keyla

While Doc talks to Creed, I give them some privacy and head across the hall to check in with my brother and his mates and find out what our plan is for the day.

"Princess Nakeyla."

The Viking on guard duty looks identical to Rhylan but their scents are not the same. "Hello, Vikarus."

"Where do you think you're going?"

Both his choice of words as well as the tone of his voice make me bristle. "If it's any business of yours, I'm headed across the hall to the Auburn Suite to see my brother and the quint."

He makes like he's considering it and then nods. "Very well. You may proceed."

"Alrighty then, thanks." I take my leave and knock on the door across the hall. "Everybody decent. Little sister doesn't want her retinas burned out."

Jaxx opens the door and grins. "Decent is subjective and

depends on how high your standards are. All I can promise is that we are clothed."

"I'll take that as a win, cowboy." I prop onto my tiptoes and kiss his cheek as I head inside. When he closes the door behind me, I throw my thumb over my shoulder. "FYI, we've got Vik the dick on duty today."

Kotah comes to hug me and walks me deeper into the suite. Brant has music blasting out of his phone and I make a face. "What's with the volume, Bear? Missing your days of bar crawls and raves?"

He chuckles, his brawny chest bouncing with amusement. "You know me, sista. I like to feel my tunes vibrate in my lungs."

Weird.

I'm about to ask Kotah why he's acting strangely when Lukas comes up to me with an electronics wand. He passes it in front of me and behind and then down my arms and each side.

I meet my brother's gaze and he points at Jaxx tipping a lamp back to show me a black chip under the shade and Hawk points to a picture on the wall and a vase on the bookshelf.

Awesome. We've been bugged.

When? I mouth. Lukas swept both their suite and ours when he first arrived.

When did someone get the chance to bug things?

Calli tips her hand against her mouth and then points to her temple. During the drink and think last night?

Yeah, maybe.

A horrifying thought hits me and I turn and point at our suite. Pulling my phone out, I type out a note. *Is our suite bugged? Does the queen know about Rhylan and Creed's mating?*

Hawk takes the phone and types back, *Not sure yet. We just found these. We need to head over and check.*

Lukas tucks his gear back into his duffle and zips a false bottom before slinging it over his shoulder. Then I lead him and the quint out to return to the royal suite.

"Problem, Princess?" Vikarus asks.

"No, why? We're just checking on the boys before we leave for Rames and Travon to make first contact."

"About that," the dragon says, offering us a cocky grin. "I'm afraid all excursions have been put on hold for the moment by order of the queen. It seems there might be a security threat. Until the queen's guard has things ironed out, it won't be safe for your brother and his mates to leave the castle."

Hawk grins. "In case you missed the part where Calli is the legendary Phoenix Guardian of the Fae and we are her quint, let me assure you, we'll be just fine."

Vik shrugs. "Sorry. I enforce the orders. I don't make them."

There's no scent of lying in the air, but somehow, I feel like *we* are the security threat he's talking about. Does he know about his brother and Creed? Would he say something if he did? Wouldn't he be upset? He couldn't be that much of an ass that he'd allow the queen to harm Rhy, could he?

While I'm considering that, four heavily-armed guards take a position at the end of the corridor—two facing our way and two facing toward the castle beyond.

"Well," Calli says, pressing her hand against my back and urging me toward the suite. "I guess we'll consider it a rain day and amuse ourselves in the royal suite, won't we?"

Shutting ourselves inside, I meet the gaze of the others and the hair on the nape of my neck stands on end. "Oh, damn. I suddenly feel sick."

Creed

I hear Keyla say she's feeling ill as Doc and I step into the suite to join her and her family. She does look a little pale and I begin to worry. "Are you all right, Little Wolf? Do you want to lie down?"

"No. I think Calli's right. I think we should celebrate our mating and stay in to enjoy the day together."

I'm confused by the mental energies in the room. What Keyla is saying doesn't in any way match the vibrations I'm getting off them.

Keyla turns to me and the mental connection we share opens. Strangely, she's able to do that. I'm the mind fae. Ordinarily, it would be me who initiates conversation. I suspect her ability has something to do with the magic of the soul-searing and our bonding.

Or she's simply a wonder.

The Auburn Suite has been bugged. It seems the queen's need to chip things continues to haunt us.

Jaxx, Kotah, and Brant put on some music and start chatting about powerful motorcycles. Keyla points to Lukas who extricates a black wand from a duffle bag and starts sweeping the room. I catch on quickly.

Doc gestures to Lukas and shrugs.

I extend the conversation to loop him in. *The quint's suite was fitted with listening devices.*

Doc frowns. *The jokes on them. Bugging their suite likely just gave the queen and her men an 'hours of sex' soundtrack.*

Yeah, and I hope her ears bled, Keyla snaps. *But more importantly. If we've been bugged too, there's a real chance that things are about to go very badly for us... depending on what she heard.*

There's not an ounce of honor in that woman, I say... and then it hits me. *Rhylan.*

She nods. *If she knows about him mating you and that his allegiance is in question, it might not be a coincidence she took him with her today and left us Vikarus.*

A wave of dizziness hits as the blood rushes from my head. *Fuck. I think he suspected something. When he was here, he kept saying the mistake was his and he wanted me to have a good life with the two of you.*

Dillan and Keyla both frown.

Lukas holds up three fingers and points to various points around the room.

"Hey, girlfriend," Calli says, calling our attention toward the kitchen. "Have you got any snacks left from last night? This baby is hungry, and I don't last long without something in my tummy."

Hawk points to Lukas's duffle bag and then back toward the bedroom.

Doc and Keyla catch on faster than I do. Then again, they've been through this before. Keyla jogs off with Calli to the kitchen while Doc retreats into our suite to pack a bag.

Hawk points to his head and then to mine and I understand what he wants. Normally mind fae don't create mental connections with anyone other than their closest contacts, but I have a feeling the quint is going to be incredibly important in my life.

Opening a mental connection is the work of a thought and then, the avian is in my mind. *We've got at least four guards plus the dragon in the hall outside. I'd bet my balls there are more ready to move in. Keyla and Doc are vulnerable to attack. If we can avoid a head-on conflict, I'd prefer it. Windows, roof... what are our options here?*

My mind is spinning. Is this happening? *My father built an escape corridor that leads to the King's suite and then down to the basement but after my second attempt at getting away, the dragons found it and had it blocked and sealed by magic.*

Where is it? I'll have Lukas take a look.

I point and head into my bedroom. Opening the wall to my hidden closet, I swipe the hangers to the side and press on the center of what looks like an ornamental panel. It pops open and I swing the panel aside, exposing an opening about two feet square.

Hawk frowns at the bars blocking the entry and nods. *Pack whatever you can't live without. Your time as her prisoner has come to its end.*

I won't run away and leave that bitch with my quadrant. I'd rather die here fighting.

Hawk drops his chin and smiles. *Oh, we're not running. We're making a strategic retreat while we find your dragon and your sister. Once we've secured them, we'll be back.*

I swallow. For two years I've dreamed about the day I would rise up and reclaim my life.

Now, it seems to be happening too fast.

Keyla rushes in and hugs me. *It's going to be fine. You haven't seen the quint in action yet, but we couldn't have a stronger backup force. Come. Grab a few things and add them to our go-bag.*

I grab a pair of pants and a couple of shirts and when I get to my dresser, I stop and stare at the top left drawer.

What is it? Keyla's internal voice carries with it such genuine concern for me I hate myself for even thinking what I'm thinking.

Hawk said to grab things I can't live without... and there's something... but I don't want to hurt you.

Keyla's expression softens. *Gather what you need. You won't hurt me.*

I open the drawer and look at the collection of things that represent another time—another love. *I wish I had time to go through this with you and explain it properly.*

Keyla's curves press against my side and her warmth eases me. *She was part of you. There's nothing you need to explain or defend or worry about.*

I wonder for a moment how she knows these are Bloom's things but then I remember. This drawer hasn't been opened for two years, everything inside it is preserved like a tomb. *You can smell her?*

Keyla nods. *You told me the other day she smelled like sweet summer blossoms. You're right. It's a lovely scent.*

I feel so disloyal... to Bloom for moving on and to Keyla for not moving on. *I'm sorry. I shouldn't have this here. Not now. It's wrong.*

Keyla turns me by the hips and smiles up at me. *You loved her and she loved you. It would be wrong* not *to cherish your memories. Now, what is it you want to bring with you? All of it?*

I swipe my fingers under my eyes and pull out the pendant she always wore. *Just this.*

That's beautiful. Keyla leans in and brushes a gentle fingertip over the glossy gold and black surface.

It's the insignia of the earth guardians. Bloom never took it off, but I couldn't let Laryssa's men take it when they took her body away.

I'm sure she's thankful you kept it safe. Do you want me to help you put it on?

You really don't mind?

Her smile makes my eyes sting. She takes it from my palm and reaches up to kiss my cheek. *I really don't. In fact, I think it's only right that you wear it. She was with you when this all began. She should be with you when we end Laryssa's hold on you and your quadrant. We're going to avenge her death, your parents', and everyone else who was lost.*

Keyla finishes with the clasp at the back of my neck, and I turn to hug her. Wrapping her in my arms, I tilt my head and press my face against the silk of her hair. *You never fail to surprise me. The universe gave me what I need. I hope you can say the same about me someday.*

Her hands against my back pull me tight, crushing the pliable mounds of her breasts against my chest. *Why wait for someday? We're building something amazing. I believe that to the depths of my soul.*

A loud crash in the living room has us jogging out to see

what the hell is going on. Vikarus and six guards have forced their way into my suite.

"What the hell, Vik? What's this about?"

Vik points to Brant, Kotah, Jaxx, and Calli who are coiled to spring. "Take them into custody."

"What? Why?"

"We don't need to explain ourselves to you," Vik says, nodding toward my guests.

"No," I snap, raising my hands and dropping the soldiers to the ground with a thought.

"Holy fuck," Brant says, glancing around, wide-eyed. "Did you do that? Did we know he can do that?"

Vik turns to glare. "How long have you had your powers back? Does my brother know? Is that why Laryssa's mad at him?"

"You knew she was mad at him and you let her take him away without warning him?"

He raises his weapon and points it at me. "Rhy's a big boy. He's been acting weird lately and asking about things he shouldn't be asking about. Is that you? Have you been manipulating him?"

I pull Vik's cognitive plug and he drops to the carpet with the others.

Hawk steps out of the bedroom and looks at the downed guards. "All right then. Tie them up. Lock the door so no one else comes in. And let's make tracks. Lukas opened our exit."

Keyla runs and pulls on her shoes. "Destiny awaits."

I draw a deep breath. There's no turning back now.

Tucking Bloom's pendant under my shirt for safekeeping, I send the universe my thanks. I may have lost one love to Laryssa's violence, but I won't lose another. With Keyla, Doc, and my newfound family at my side, I finally have what I need to reclaim my life.

We're coming Rhy. Hang on.

CHAPTER FIFTEEN

Rhylan

𝓛 aryssa is a lot of things: a manipulator of good people, a weak coward who hides behind the strength and threat of others, a cunning opportunist, and a heartlessly driven, single-minded bitch. What she is not, and never has been, is a keen observer of the strengths of the people she opposes.

She sees herself as the biggest and baddest and with her witch and her army and her dragon enforcers at her side, everyone else is deemed irrelevant—insignificant bugs to be flicked away and squashed.

And while it's been effective in securing her crown, it won't be enough for her to keep it.

The people around her aren't loyal, they're simply watching their backs.

I'm no different.

She wanted lethal thugs behind her and bought our service from Shadowcaster. In her mind, she owns us. In my mind, she overestimates her hold on our loyalty.

"You are quiet this morning, Rhylan." Laryssa exits the StoneHaven Citadel, her briefcase latched to her wrist. After almost two hours of standing around outside the door to the Journey Chamber, she's emerged with a wicked smile on her face. I have no idea what's in that case, but I would bet it's nothing good. "Have a lot on your mind, do you?"

"As always, Majesty," I hold my hand out to a small group of people to keep them at a distance while we make our way back to the three-car conveyance. The pedestrians stop, allowing us to pass, and we continue on our way unhindered.

"Your twin doesn't seem to suffer from the same mental toiling."

I chuckle and open the rear door to the oversized truck. "No, Majesty. Vikarus doesn't feel the need to think beyond the moment he's in."

"But you do?"

I hold her fingers and help her slide in. When she's settled with her briefcase on her lap, I close her door, check the sight-lines for any cause for concern and then round the truck. The other two guards take the front seats and I climb in the back with the queen.

"Quadrant security and the security of the prince involve many shifting factors. Since the rift was opened and Prince Creed was soul-seared and invited the Wolf King into the castle, there have been many new considerations to juggle."

She nods. "Yes, many new considerations. You've failed to assert yourself as the man of power in more than one instance this week."

The truck pulls away from the entrance of the historic center and I watch the old, ivy-covered buildings pass by. "I won't deny that. Nakotah is an intelligent man driven to unite the realms and safeguard his sister. There have been instances where if I stopped him or Creed from saying or doing things it would've become combative."

"And what's wrong with combative?"

Her tone warns me to choose my words wisely. "Nothing, if the people on the receiving end are standing in direct opposition but the Wolf King and his mates aren't your enemies."

"Aren't they?"

Well, they are, but I'm not about to throw that in her face. "They've never made any overt move to oppose your authority."

"And if they did, what would you do about it?"

"I'd bring it to you. Until something like that happens, you made it clear to keep things friendly while you assess their usefulness in furthering your cause."

"Did I?"

"Yes."

"So, you're saying it's because of me and my desires that they have been given a key to the city."

I shrug. "If you're unhappy with their presence and their access to the city, put a stop to it, Majesty. You are the queen."

She offers me a cold smile. "Exactly, right, Dragon. I am. Would you mind handing me your weapon?"

My mind balks at that. "I'm sorry, what?"

"Your sidearm. I'd like to examine it."

My dragon rears its head and an eerie calm settles over me. I breathe deeply, searching the air for the smell of deceit or anxiety from the guards up front.

"Rhylan? Don't make me ask you again."

Knowing this will bite me in the balls but unable to see a way out of it other than to obey, I unholster my weapon and hand it to the queen.

After setting it on top of her briefcase, she looks me over and frowns. "The way you hesitated makes me feel as though you don't trust me, Dragon... or perhaps you are afraid of me."

I answer as honestly as I can. "I know you're displeased with me and you are lethal to those who fail you. I would be a fool not to recognize your power over me and the position it puts me in to surrender my weapon."

"You always were the smart one. Yesterday, I asked the same thing of your twin and Vikarus handed me his sidearm without blinking an eye."

I swallow. "As we discussed. He's not one to assess a situation. He's reactive, not proactive."

"You're right. Vikarus is a soldier dedicated to doing his duty and not much more beyond that." Laryssa runs a pointed fingernail along the silver sheen of my weapon and smiles. "I admit, I prefer blind obedience."

Slecking hell. My dragon is ascending fast and I fight to hold him back. Shifting in the truck next to the queen would be a bad idea... unless it wouldn't.

I turn my gaze on the queen and she sees her demise on the horizon. The stench of panic and fury hit the moment before I'm blasted twice at close range.

My murderous gaze spins toward the guard in the passenger's seat up front and I reach forward. I backhand his weapon through the front windshield as my dragon claws pierce the flesh and bone of my human hand. Gripping the column of his throat, I squeeze with crushing force. The snap of bone is incredibly satisfying.

In a move driven by adrenaline more than thought, I kick the truck door out, grab the queen, and drag her from the car. "You shouldn't have done that, Laryssa," I say, my voice vibrating with the instability of needing to shift.

Two shots catch me in the back and I spin.

Damn it. The driver shot me with electrical pulses to negate my shift. The other guard had his weapon set to kill. Except, kill a human or fae is different than kill a dragon.

Still, it slecking hurt, and I'm seriously injured.

"Let go of me, Rhylan," the queen sputters. "How dare you betray me."

I grunt, hiking her up to grab her around the waist to use as a shield. Gripping the briefcase attached to her wrist, she swings wildly, pelting me with it.

"You've got that backward, bitch. I was loyal. You tried to have me killed. The betrayal is yours."

We're still on the Citadel grounds, the paved roadway lined by manicured greenspaces and walkways leading to other buildings.

All three trucks have stopped and guards are oozing out of trucks looking baffled.

"Sorry boys," I say, meeting the gaze of nine guys I've worked with for the past two years. "Laryssa decided to end my employment and thought ambushing me in transit was the best way to do it."

Laryssa gives up on beating me with her leather case and takes to flailing like an insane cat. Her claws and teeth slice at my skin as she loses her mind. "How dare you," she screeches. "I own you."

I chuff. "If that's what you thought, it's your mistake. Too bad for you."

Her men are fanning out and I shake my head. "Don't bother, guys. Make one move on me, and I snap her neck and we all go back to the castle to tell Creed he can have his life back."

"You'd like that," she hisses. "This wouldn't have happened if you weren't sleeping with Creed."

I register the shock and revulsion on the faces of men I respect, and I stand taller. "I won't deny it. Creed and I are together. I've always thought he was the rightful ruler of Dornte, but I never would've broken my vow to Laryssa or ignored my duty. Betrayal isn't my thing."

Stepping back, I assess my chances of escape. Between the electrical pulses and the damage taken in the car, I won't be shifting and flying out of here.

I don't need to look at my side to realize there's a hole in me somewhere. The sticky warmth pissing down my hip and thigh tells me it's bad.

The odds of me against ten decently trained men aren't good. The only thing keeping them from coming at me is the purple-skinned bitch going apeshit in my arms. With nowhere to go, I might as well go all in and end the bitch.

If I'm to die here, at least I'll know I did my part.

Reaching around her shoulder, I grip her throat and start to squeeze.

In the truck, when I crushed the guard's windpipe, it was the work of a moment. Even in this form, I have the strength of my wild side. No matter how hard I try, I can't seem to snap Laryssa's neck.

"You'd kill me after everything I've done for you?"

"In a heartbeat, bitch. So, why aren't you dead?"

Laryssa lets off a long, twisted cackle. "Because I don't underestimate people nearly as much as you think I do. Everyone in my service has been conditioned by my witch's magic. You can't kill me. I'm untouchable."

Slecking hell. I hate the sound of that.

"Move in boys. There's nothing he can do to me. Rush him and kill him."

Her guards look cautious at first.

Then they aggress.

Shit. Shit. Shit. There's only one move. If I stay, I die. I've got to go. Backing up, I scan the grounds behind me.

I've got thirty feet of open space before the first bit of cover. And when I say cover, that's overstating things. There are two, spindly white birch trees with a bench. It's not even a cement bench. It's slatted wood which won't do me much good.

Beyond that. I've got another fifty feet before I get to a building.

Still, there are no options.

Only the possibility of distraction.

Gripping her arm with one hand and the chain of her brief-case with the other, I yank with all my strength. the metal ring slices through her wrist like a knife through butter and the queen lets off an ear-piercing scream.

Turning, I race for those two twigs growing behind the bench. Arms pumping, legs propelling me forward, I focus on the only chance I've got.

Laser bolts zing past my head as I run.

I duck, cursing as I close the distance to the pathetic excuse for cover. The fiery sizzle of one shot catches me in the ass.

I hiss, my footing faltering, but I ignore the pain. All those years of being the favored punching bag of our brood have left me rather unaffected by pain.

I reach the two little trees and slide in behind them, panting for breath. Normally, I wouldn't be winded, but I've lost a lot of blood and the world is a little spinny.

Casting a quick glance back, I'm happy to see half the guards tending to the queen. She's doubled over screaming and shit... there's a lot of blood.

I hold up the briefcase and chuckle at the mauve hand dangling from the end of the chain. I may not be able to kill her, but that is almost as good.

The guards who opted to come after me instead of securing the queen are approaching fast.

I curse, pushing off the trees, and set my sights on the building.

I haven't made it twenty feet when someone hits my back and I'm knocked to the grass.

"Stay down," a man shouts, rolling on top of me as the world bursts into a fiery inferno.

I close my eyes and wince. The heat is excruciating. The guy on top of me must be getting fried alive.

After a moment, the heat is gone and I shiver at the plummet in temperature. The weight on my back is released and many hands are gripping me and scooping me off the ground.

"I've got you, Rhy," Creed says, stuffing me into the back of a van. "Where are you hurt?"

Flopping against the metal floor, I try to catch my breath. "Side, ass, shoulder."

"Let me see him," another voice says.

Creed backs away and I'm about to protest when he shifts to kneel by my head. His bear, Dillan, takes his place at my side. My shirt is no match for the bear's strength and a second later, he's probing the damage to my hip.

"How is he, Doc?" Creed asks.

"He's lost a lot of blood, but Calli's tears will save his life. Pass me that medical bag."

Creed shifts to do as he's asked and then a glorious white wolf jumps in the back of the van followed by a dark brown and silver one.

A moment later the front doors open, and slam shut. "Are we good to skedaddle?" the southern jaguar says.

"Yeah," Doc says. "Get us out of here, Jaxx."

The engine revs and the world rocks. There's too much happening and I can't focus.

The gentle touch of a female's hand cups my cheek and then Creed's wolf is looking down over me. "It's okay now, Dragon. Close your eyes. We've got you. You're safe."

The last thing I remember is shaking my head. "Open the briefcase."

CHAPTER SIXTEEN

Creed

$\mathcal{A}$ s Rhy falls slack against the floor of the van, I check with Doc and he shakes his head. "He's simply passed out. Don't panic. Grab the vial in the side pocket of our duffle and we'll get him fixed up."

I do the honors and unzip the glass vial of Calli's phoenix tears from where I saw him stash them a few hours ago.

Has it only been that long since Rhy punched me in the face?

I unscrew the top and shift my position to get a better look at the damage he sustained.

"By the scent of things, the worst is this one here on his side. Cover the wound and let the liquid soak in, then we'll roll him and do his ass and shoulder."

"Hey, look, a souvenir!" Brant chuckles as he holds up a leather briefcase. I blink at the hand still attached to the security cuff. "Do you guys need a hand back there? I could lend you a hand. Many hands make light work."

Doc rolls his eyes and points to Rhylan's pants. "Ignore my

brother and undo the dragon's pants. I need to see the damage done."

Brant snorts. "Nah, you don't fool us, Doc. You just want to see your new mate's ass."

"Here's an idea," Doc says, scowling. "Open the fucking briefcase and stop being such a comedian. Our mate was moments away from being killed and still he wanted to ensure we ended up with that case. It might be important."

I hadn't thought about it like that, but yeah. "That's Laryssa's briefcase. She takes it with her whenever she's on one of her fact-finding missions."

"Okay," Jaxx says, pulling into a parking lot and shifting the truck into park. "We'll pause here and see what we've got. Kotah, you run back and check on Calli, Hawk, and Lukas. Bring them back here and maybe we'll know our next step by the time you return."

Keyla opens the two folding back doors of the van and lets her brother out. "Be safe, Wolf King. Bite some ass." Instead of hopping back inside and closing the door, she checks out the surroundings and smiles. "Oh, StoneHaven is wonderful. Look at these buildings."

"I'm too wound up about Rhylan for site-seeing at the moment," I mutter under my breath.

"Easy," Doc whispers. "Don't take your mood out on our girl."

"Sorry. She doesn't understand. She doesn't have the same connection with Rhy as I do."

Doc chuckles. "It's not that. It's you who doesn't understand. We've been around healings with Calli's tears enough to realize the moment they are in play, there's no danger. He's good. The danger is over."

I want to believe that, but my heart is still hammering hard in my chest. "I hope you're right."

Doc finishes cleaning the singed skin on Rhylan's ass and

then points to the wound. "I am. A couple of drops here and he'll be as good as new."

With only his shoulder left, the two of us make quick work of finishing off the healing. When we're done, Doc spreads a blanket out on the floor of the van, and we move him and cover him up.

"I'll stay with him," Doc says. "You go see what we got in that briefcase."

I hesitate for a moment, but the reassurance in Doc's smile spurs me on. "All right but let me know when he wakes up."

"Will do."

Shuffling to the back of the van, I drop down and look around to where Jaxx and Brant are spreading papers and bound folders across a patch of grass with Keyla. "What did we get?"

"We're still sorting that out," Jaxx says. "A lot of names and notes."

"You'll probably know better than us what some of this means," Brant says.

"Incoming," Keyla says, reaching forward and laying her arms across the papers.

Calli's mighty wingspan churns the air around us as the phoenix drops from the sky and shifts back to human. Unlike the other wildlings I know, she doesn't flash clothes on and, instead, stands at the back of the van totally naked.

Keyla catches me looking and smiles. "You'll live longer if you keep your eyes front, my prince."

My cheeks flush hot and I'm not sure if she's suggesting that she's the danger or Calli's mates, but it's not worth me asking. "Calliope is a beautiful woman, but I was actually wondering why she doesn't flash on clothes like the rest of you."

"Calli was born human," Jaxx says. "She missed out on the genetic lottery with heightened senses and the magic to manifest clothing."

Hawk grabs a backpack from the van and pulls out a t-shirt, yoga pants, and a pair of sneakers. "She has an entire wardrobe of fire-resistant clothing but has almost mastered regulating her body temperature to not need it anymore."

Kotah trots in to join us and shifts back looking content after his run. "How's Rhylan?"

"Nothing some Calli tears couldn't handle," Keyla says. "Are we all clear?"

Hawk nods. "The queen's men evacuated her and raced off as soon as Calli started laying down a blanket of fire."

"Where's Lukas?"

"Here." The military man scans the files and frowns. "What are we looking at?"

Jaxx sits back on his heels. "From a first look-see, Laryssa has a few travelers on the payroll to keep tabs on key players in our realm. One of which is your baby brother, hotness."

Hawk's expression darkens. "She's in communication with Hunter?"

"Uh-huh. And by the messages she's been passing, it seems like she's probing to find out if the plans she made with daddy dearest are still viable."

Hawk arches an imperious brow. "Not if I find Hunter first."

"This is interesting," Keyla says, opening a blue folder. "These correspondences are all about building a lead vault. There are material requisitions, and schematics, and notes about securing the thickest sheets of metal she can find. What do you think she'd store in a lead vault?"

"Kryptonite?" Brant asks.

"What's kryptonite?" I ask, confused.

"Ignore him," Hawk says. "He's spouting off and cracking wise."

"Then if that wasn't a real guess, I have one."

"What's that?"

"My sister. During the Wars of Power, locking mind fae

within lead-lined rooms was considered the most effective way to hold them prisoner."

Keyla hands me the folder and I skim through the specifications. "The timing matches up with when Rhylan says Honor was recaptured."

Calli shuffles in and looks over my shoulder. "Is there a manifest for delivery? A drop-off address? Anything that could tell us where she's being held?"

"Unfortunately, no," I say, flipping through the pages. "Nothing like that."

Something about the mental energy of Lukas catches my attention. "What are you thinking?"

Lukas points toward the buildings. "If this is where the traveler equipment is located and where Honor spent almost a year during her escape from Laryssa, someone must've been helping her and keeping her whereabouts a secret. I'm thinking that while Hawk and the quint go through those folders, you, Keyla, Calli, and I go try to find out who."

"I'm game," Calli says. "If it helps to find Riley, I'm game for anything."

I look back at the van. "Give me two minutes to check on Rhylan first. If Doc thinks he's improving and is stable, we'll go."

Keyla

After Doc assures Creed that Rhylan will survive, we cross the grounds of the StoneHaven Citadel. He's still shaken and torn about leaving but he's equally anxious to find his sister. I slide my hand against Creed's palm and squeeze. "Are you okay?"

"Yeah. I know you and Doc say the phoenix tears will heal Rhy right up, but he hasn't woken up yet."

Calli chuckles. "Hey, there aren't too many things I rock at in the supernatural world, but healing I can do. Trust us. He'll be fine."

I squeeze his palm and open our mental connection to speak to him mind-to-mind. *Hear my words and feel the truth in them. Rhy will be fine. Between the tears and Doc taking care of him, there's nothing to worry about.*

Then why hasn't he woken up?

Living and healing doesn't negate the fact that he lost a lot of blood. He's been through a great deal of trauma lately, not only physically but emotionally as well. Maybe he needs a moment to regroup.

I hope you're right.

I am. And hey, once he wakes up, he might need to replenish some of that blood. He might need to feed on his mate.

I chuckle as a surge of his sexual arousal bursts into the air. *Mmm, like that idea, do you?*

He ducks his head, his pale cheeks pink. *Sorry.*

Don't apologize. Rhylan sucking on your neck while palming you is hand's down one of the most erotic images I've ever seen.

To punctuate my point, I call up the picture of the two of them in my mind. His footing falters and I laugh. *I told you.*

He pulls himself up and stops walking, gathering my wrists in his hands as he closes his eyes. *I... uh, didn't realize the show was so...*

Hot?

Now I'm back to being mortified your family witnessed that.

I laugh and call up the memory of the naked nacho fiasco for him to see. Jaxx in his apron. Brant naked and punching Hawk. Kotah holding Calli's hair as she puked into the sink. Mother's face as she took in the sights. *See. Nothing to panic about.*

"How are you showing me these things, Little Wolf?" he asks.

"What do you mean? It's your gift."

He shakes his head, his silver hair catching in the sunlight. "No. My gift allows me to open a channel of communication and show *you* things, but you opened that channel and showed *me* images. It's not a two-way street."

"I don't know what to tell you. I didn't do it until you did it first with me. Now, it just happens when I think about it." I shrug and catch Lukas and Calli, milling around waiting to continue. "Oh, sorry. Yep. We're ready."

The four of us are heading toward the building with the towering dome on top when a tiny man flutters down from a third-story window and lands in the grass in front of us. He's only three feet tall, but he's almost as broad as he is tall and his muscles roll and bulge as much as Brant's. He's also got a full beard that hangs to his belly and bushy eyebrows that look like fuzzy caterpillars.

Lukas draws his gun and Calli steps in front of us, but the man doesn't seem to notice. His attention is solidly focused on—

"Prince Creed? Is that you, Highness?"

Creed raises a hand to ward off Lukas and Calli's concern. "It's fine. He means me no harm."

That seems to bring his attention to the danger he was in a moment ago had his actions been deemed hostile. "Oh, no, sire. No harm to you or yours. Apologies. Brizbin is just so thankful you've finally come."

"Finally?" he asks.

"Yes. Your sister said you would... and Brizbin waited. When weeks and then months passed, I wondered if you might never come, but a promise made is a promise kept, she said."

He nods and looks at Calli. "That's another one of her favorites."

Calli's grin is as bright and excited as I've ever seen. "Yep. Riley said that all the time. It must be her. That means, she's alive and we're going to find her."

"Oh, yes, Princess Honor is alive, sire. Brizbin checks on her every day and every night. No question."

Creed spins, his gaze widening. "My sister? You check on Honor?"

The wee man nods. "Yes, sire. Brizbin never forgot his promise. Not once. Not ever."

"And what promise is that, Brizbin?" I ask.

The man turns his gaze to me and smiles. "You're the Human Realm Princess. Brizbin saw you on the updates. You soul-seared with His Highness."

I catch Creed's growing agitation on our open mental channel and try to speed this along. "What did you promise Honor, Brizbin? Are you supposed to give Prince Creed a message? If you check that she's all right, you must know where she is, yes?"

"Yes, and no, and sort of," the man says.

Creed rubs his fingers over his face, and I step between him and the gnome and turn him a little to face me. "It's time for you to fulfill your promise to Honor, Brizbin. What did she ask of you?"

"It's up there. Come, Brizbin will show you."

The man pushes off the ground and flies toward the open window he came out of.

When he disappears and doesn't come back out, Creed curses. "I take it we're supposed to follow him?"

Calli chuckles as we strike off toward the entrance of the building. "He's an odd little guy, isn't he?"

Creed grunts. "He's a miner gnome. They're all a little odd. Good people though. Hard-working. Honest people."

"Then a good champion for your sister to enlist to her cause."

Lukas grabs the handle of the front door and swings it for Creed to grab and then reclaims the lead up the three flights of steps and right off the landing.

I'm beginning to think we'll need to knock on all the doors

when one opens down the hall and Brizbin pokes his head out. "Hurry. Brizbin too excited for you to dally."

Creed mutters something unkind but I forgive his frustration. He's been desperate to find his sister for years.

The room Brizbin takes us to is an ordinary office. I scan the bookcases, desk, guest chairs, credenza. Nothing here screams anything about rescuing a kidnapped princess or how this little man got involved.

"Lock the door, please, soldier," he says, pointing at Lukas before going to the window and closing us in. He pulls the blinds, grins, and then rolls his desk chair out from behind his desk. "Come. Brizbin shows you."

Shifting a vase on a low shelf of the bookcase, he flicks a switch, and then the hum of hydraulics sounds. A soft vibration rumbles beneath my feet and then stops. "Come. Come."

With more hustle than I expect from the guy, he shuffles around the desk and ducks out of sight.

"Follow that gnome," Calli says, grinning.

Creed takes the lead, then Calli, then me, and then Lukas covers our butts.

The floor behind the desk has drifted out of the way, leaving an opening and stairs leading to the floor below. The room down there is narrow and dark and if the floorplan is similar, runs from the outside wall toward the central corridor in a narrow strip.

"I take it that's not a dental chair," Calli says, pointing at the beige, leather recliner hooked up to what looks like a brass satellite dish.

"No," Creed says, examining the connections and the readout screen. "It's a traveler's bed but it's been modified."

"For long-term," Brizbin says. "Princess Honor recalibrated it for long-term."

"Winner!" Calli says. "Houston, we have lift off."

Creed and Brizbin look confused.

Lukas and I chuckle.

"She's excited for the confirmation that Honor is Riley," I say. "So, what's the promise you made her?"

The gnome grins. "Brizbin promised Princess Honor that Prince Creed would travel in and find her."

I stare at the table and a wave of nausea hits me. "No. That's a terrible idea."

CHAPTER SEVENTEEN

Creed

I read the concern in Keyla's gaze and feel how erratically her synapses start firing. I'm touched. She is genuinely upset at the idea of me linking up to this traveler bed. What she doesn't understand is that I would do anything to find Honor.

Easing forward, I set my hands on her hips. "It's fine. Traveler beds are built specifically for mind fae. My natural physiology makes it as simple a process as it is for you to put bread in your poppers and toast them."

"That's a toaster, not a popper, and I still don't like the idea of you attaching your brain to a computer."

"Trust me, Little Wolf. The process poses no danger to me. I'll be fine."

"You mentioned finding her," Calli says to Brizbin. "What does that mean? How does Creed connecting with this machine help find her?"

Brizbin flutters the four copper wings on his back and

hovers up to tap the machine's operational screen. "The princess was connected to this machine very often for a very long time."

"Yeah," Calli says, "Almost a year."

He shakes his head. "She stayed with us for almost a year, but she wasn't always connected. When her human host was in REM sleep, she woke up here to eat and walk the grounds to stay healthy and strong."

"Is that why Riley was impossible to wake up?" Calli asks. "I always joked the big quake would come, and California would drop off the map and she'd sleep through it."

Brizbin nods. "That is why."

I hop up on the table and pull the cap on. "Did she leave her imprint for me to follow?"

"She did. She remained connected to the bed always and when she stepped away, she used a mobile unit to stay connected."

I meet Calli's gaze and smile. "That way, if you needed her in the night, she'd be alerted that she had to wake up and she could get back here and send her consciousness back to you."

"Or," Calli says looking annoyed. "She could've just told me what was going on."

I shake my head. "No. She was already breaking a dozen timeline protocols by interfering with your life, if she exposed who she was and why she was there, it could've altered how you responded to your destiny and your quint."

"You mean like not clubbing Jaxx in the head and almost killing him? Honestly, I could live without that."

I sense the sharp pain in her memories and my heart goes out to her. "Everything that happened brought you to where you are now. All is well."

Calli rolls her eyes. "We'll agree to disagree. So, here and now. You're going to lay down, close your eyes, and then what?"

"If her imprint is intact and she was wearing a mobile unit when she was recaptured, this bed should be able to connect with her last memories and possibly lead me to where they took her."

"Which may or may not be where they have her now," Lukas says. "They might have moved her."

I nod. "But you're forgetting that Brizbin's been checking on her morning and night."

The gnome nods. "That is correct, sire. Her signal is strong. She isn't communicating, but I believe that is because something is blocking her, not because she is harmed."

"Blocked, like her being locked in a lead vault?" Keyla asks.

I nod. "That would do it."

Keyla looks at me and frowns. "Swear to me that this is one-hundred percent safe, and I have nothing to worry about."

I trail my fingers along the soft line of her jaw and marvel at how her mental impulses fire with affection. Her passion and devotion to me is truly humbling. "To say it is completely safe would be a lie and you'd smell it immediately. Let's consider it ninety percent safe, and I'll assure you that you have nothing to worry about. These beds are made for mind fae. I'm more than that—I'm a Mind Guardian. I have far more power than anyone else using them and will be fine."

She leans in and presses her lips against mine. "I'll be right here, waiting for you when you get back."

"That's the best incentive I could ask for. I'll return before you can miss me."

"Too late. I already do."

I chuckle and lie flat, closing my eyes.

"Are you ready to commence, sire?"

"Ready, Brizbin. Send me off."

Rhylan

My consciousness rises in slow, ebbing waves. I feel oddly tingly and very tired. I shift my legs and realize I'm naked and wrapped in a coarse blanket. What the hell... I remember then. Laryssa turned on me. My eyes snap open and I pike up to sit.

"Easy, Dragon," Doc says, holding up his hands. "You're recovering from three laser blasts and the loss of a lot of blood."

"Where's Creed? He was here, wasn't he? Did I imagine that?"

"He was here," Doc says, claiming my arm and checking his watch to track my pulse. "He and Keyla went with Lukas and Calli to find out what the queen was doing here."

"She wanted to reconnect with the avian's brother and assess her footing to continue with her plans in the Human Realm."

"Yeah," Hawk says from outside. He rounds the open door and looks inside. "Glad you're still with us, Dragon. You did well to get away with what you did."

Brant joins his mate and chuckles. "And ripping off her hand is classic. I would've loved to see her face."

"Me too, actually," I say, replaying the moment in my mind. "Sadly, I was standing behind her and started running the moment I yanked the briefcase free. I didn't even realize I had her hand until I paused for cover."

Doc finishes with his checkup and sits back on his heels. "I don't like your pulse rate. It's sluggish even though you just woke in a panic. How are you feeling?"

"I'm good," I say waving away his concern. "Dragons get like that when we need to feed. Losing that much blood, it's not surprising."

"But it's also not good, is it?"

I close my eyes and the world spins. Cutting that off quickly, I open things up and shrug. "I'm sure it'll be fine after a while."

"How sure?" Doc's gaze narrows and I know he'll assess my response for any hint of me lying.

"Yes, I need to feed, but I can wait. Vik and I have females... right, I guess I won't be feeding back at the castle anymore."

"No. I think your time there has ended."

That thought is both liberating and terrifying.

"So, without your usual food sources standing by, you'll need someone to be your blood bank, yes?"

I see the look in his eyes but... "I'm sure Creed will be back soon."

"Are you? I'm not. They went to find out about the queen's visit. Odds are, they'll be a while."

I lay back down and stare at the ceiling of the van. "That's fine. I'll wait."

"Why? I guarantee you I have blood in my veins and it's wildling blood. It's probably better for you than random females back at the castle."

"Yeah, but you saw how raw I get when I feed. Random females at the castle fulfill other needs as well as topping up my strength."

The bear arches a brow. "That's what this is about? You get horny while you feed and are holding off for what? A sense of decency? Propriety? Aloof pride? That's stupid."

"And is it less stupid that you're pissed at me for trying to do right by you?"

"Yeah, it is. Obviously, I have what you need, and not only am I worried about you as a doctor. I'm worried about you as your mate. Like it or not, we're bound by your claim on Creed. There are no more random females in your future, so welcome to your new normal."

I chuff. "My new normal doesn't have to mean me rocking cock with you in a van like a teenager."

He has the nerve to chuckle. "Let's start with the feeding and not worry where things go after that."

"I don't have to worry about it. I'm not strong enough to

hold back. Feeding is raw and intimate… I'll take more than your blood."

"Then we both know the score." Doc looks me over and dips his chin in a quick nod. "Hey, Hawk. Do you mind shutting those doors for a bit? We've got some mate business to take care of in here. And if the van's a rockin'…"

"Got it," Hawk says. "I'll knock twice on the side if you need to wrap it up."

"Good enough."

When the tin can shuts tight and the bear peels off his shirt, I shake my head. "This is a bad idea. You've got no idea—"

He barks a laugh, drops his jeans, and lowers himself onto the blanket in only his boxers. "I watched what you did to Creed when you fed off him. I can take that kind of punishment. Don't you worry about me. You just feed and take what you need."

Doc

Stupid dragon. The guy is lethargic, and his speech is starting to slur. His pulse rate has dropped from ten minutes ago which dropped from twenty minutes before that. Sure, Calli's tears are healing his wounds, but the guy needs to feed and he's too stubborn to realize it.

"Where do you want me?" I ask, shifting onto my back next to him.

He's still sitting up, glaring at me, but I don't care. To save the man's life… there's no question. Add to that fact he's our fourth—even though it's awkward and early days—I'm all in.

Reaching up, I hook my arm over his shoulder and pull him down across my chest. With a bit of shifting, I get him settled and tilt my neck away to give him my throat. "Feed from me, Dragon. Take what I'm offering."

Lacing my fingers into his hair, I pull the back of his head and force him toward my vein. His lips brush the skin on my throat. He is tentative at first, his tongue brushing a reluctant sweep over the blood racing through my jugular.

I sense his wild side rising to the fore but it's taking some coaxing.

"That's it. Feed your dragon. Forget everything outside of this van and take what you need."

"I hate that you smell so good."

"I'm your mate. What I have is yours."

The man might be weak, but the animal within is strong. Rhylan's dragon knows what it needs and isn't shy about taking it. His hands run across my bare chest and then he grips my shoulder and pushes up to climb on top of me.

I swallow and steady him, caressing his muscled back and down his uninjured side. The muscled contours of his body are sexy as hell and so is his body's natural response to whatever is happening here.

To show him I'm all right with whatever happens, I stroke over his hard cock and squeeze his length.

His dragon groans and his hips kick against my hold. The frustration of his scent is replaced by hunger.

"Yeah," I breathe. "That's right. I'm here for you."

His grip tightens and the strength of his dragon ascends further. "Take what I need? You're sure?"

Fuck. With the rugged hunger of this guy and the way he's grinding on me and laving me with his tongue, I'm hard and hungry too. "I'm sure."

With strength and speed I didn't realize he still had in him, Rhylan pushes up onto his knees and switches directions. Instead of laying on top of me with our bodies aligned, he spins around, crawls down my body, and shoves my boxers out of the way.

I scissor my legs and kick my legs free but am a little

confused. There's no time for a sixty-nine suck-off. "You need to take my vein, my man."

His dragon growls and it's a rough and possessive sound. My cock jumps against my abdomen and then he's dropping his head. It doesn't take long for me to catch up with his intentions. He's licking along the crux of my groin and nuzzling the inside of my thigh.

The femoral artery.

He's going to feed on me down— "Oh, fuck,"

The strike is fast and brutal. My body shudders and my first reaction is to push off and get some distance. I wasn't kidding when we played two truths and a lie. I'm a freaking wimp about needles. But I fight the instinct to bolt and settle. He needs this.

And if I'm being honest, now that we're here and it's happening, I want it.

Relaxing under his hold I draw a deep breath and focus on the sensation. The initial sting of being pierced has subsided and now it's all about pleasure.

"Fuck, that feels good." I send a hand along the curve of his spine and palm the round of his ass.

The dragon has an amazing ass.

The damage from his blaster wound is almost completely healed but I steer clear of it anyway. "You're rocking an impressive cock here, Dragon. I like the piercing. How about I help you with that?"

He moans and I take that as a yes.

Gripping his hips, I use my bear's strength to lift him over my shoulders. When he splits his knees, I set him down so he's straddling my head.

Damn. The scent of his arousal zaps me right in the balls, his desire thick in the air. It may be a side-effect of the feeding and not about me personally, but with the pulsing of my cock as he drinks from me—I don't care.

Gripping his cock at the base, I prop it out and take that

thick, blunt head into my mouth. His suckling stops as he goes rigid, and then he's back to drinking. My bear surges forward as he returns the attention, shifting his hand to grip my erection in turn.

"Fuck, yeah," I groan, easing off his shaft. Arching my hips, I take advantage of his vice grip. "Don't be gentle. Yeah, that's it."

Distantly, it dawns on me that this isn't about me but like Jaxx says, It's easier lettin' the cat outta the bag than it is stuffin' the thing back in.

Flicking my tongue, I toy with the metal ball piercing the crown of his cock and get a feel for what he likes. Once I get a sense of his body, I open my throat and suck him down deep.

His growl rumbles in my chest. I've never had a lover with a piercing and it's kinda fun.

As the sensations bombard, I close my eyes, and enjoy the gentle spin the world is taking. I'm on what I suspect is a bit of a blood buzz and it makes everything seem out of control and a little dangerous.

It probably is a little dangerous. He's been drinking with solid pulls for a while now. Not that I have any interest in slowing things down—I don't.

After a few more sucking gulps, he retracts his bite. I feel every fraction of an inch as he withdraws his teeth and it's a hollow victory. Then he's licking over the puncture holes with his tongue and my focus shifts back to how fucking hot this is.

"Better?" I ask, around the hot flesh of his shaft.

"Drinking you is like an infusion of strength."

"You say the sweetest things."

With the task of feeding taken care of Rhylan adjusts his position and then it's the two of us sixty-nineing like animals. Everything bursts into a fast and furious exchange of hips pumping up and down, and cocks gliding in and out. The suction has the pressure in my balls tingling and my brain misfiring and then—

My orgasm rips free and my abs clench. I thrust upward and it's lucky he's on top and can back off or I'd come straight into his stomach.

The dragon hisses, his cock kicking hard.

He comes in great spasms, his release filling my mouth in waves of salty heat. I take everything he's giving, milking him while he rides out every last moment of his orgasm.

I'm still a bit dizzy when Rhylan's body goes slack, and he tilts to the side. Rolling onto the floor of the truck, he collapses beside me.

The combined scents of our arousal create an intoxicating aroma in such an enclosed space and since the two of us needed some get-to-know-you, I figure we've made good use of our time.

Saving the guy's life is a solid foundation.

The sound of two wildlings catching their breath after a couple of fierce orgasms is almost as sexy as the sex itself. "Just what the doctor ordered," I rasp.

"You've got one hell of a bedside manner, Doc."

"I try."

It takes a moment for the adrenaline rushing through my veins to slow enough to sit up. Grabbing my duffle, I pull out my spare pants and a hoodie and toss them to him. "Are you ready to resume life?"

"Where do I begin? The life I had crumbled and the ruins were set on fire."

I chuckle. "I don't suppose ripping the queen's hand off will win you any favors in her circles, but I gotta say, I think it's funny as hell."

He chuckles and tosses me my boxers. "I wanted to do more than that. The bitch had her blood witch do something to me so I can't take her life."

"Not as dumb as she seems, then."

"No. Unfortunately not."

When we've pulled ourselves together, I open the back door of the van and we join Jaxx and Brant.

"You look better," Jaxx says, assessing the dragon.

Rhylan swallows and sends me a half-smile. "I needed to feed more than I realized."

Brant's brows arch as he tilts his head side to side, studying me. "I don't see any of those little vamp marks on your neck, my brother. Where did he sink those fangs of his into you?"

"None of your fucking business."

His deep chuckle is irritating as hell. "Touchy, touchy. Never mind, I've got a good imagination."

I flash him my middle finger and change the subject. "Where are Kotah and Hawk?"

"They were gettin' antsy about Calli and how long they've been gone. Kotah shifted to wolf and they've gone to track them down."

I turn toward the manicured grounds of the Citadel. "All right then, let's go track down our mates."

CHAPTER EIGHTEEN

Keyla

I hate seeing Creed lying there, so still. Logic dictates that if a person projects their consciousness out of their body they won't be active, but it's unnerving to see my prince lying there so lifeless.

"How long will it take for him to track Honor's memories?" I ask.

Brizbin flaps his wings and lifts himself into the air to read the readouts on the screen. "Not long. He's on his way back now."

I don't know when I've ever been so relieved.

Taking Creed's hand, I step closer to the side of the traveler bed, watching and waiting for him to wake up. When his eyes flutter open, his gaze is hazy for a moment and then focuses on me. "I told you not to worry," he says, brushing a finger over my cheek.

"I think that's a mate's prerogative."

He sits up and swings his feet to the floor. I move back to give him space to stand up but he splits his knees and pulls me against his chest. "Thank you for worrying about me. It's been a long time since anyone cared."

I rise onto my tiptoes and brush his lips with mine. "I more than care, my prince."

That earns me a soul-aching look. "Me too."

"Congratulations on your awesomeness," Calli says. "I mean that, sincerely, but can we get to the part about whether or not you found my BFF and where she is?"

Creed eases back and smiles. "I did. She's been taken to a compound in the badlands of Travon."

"Do you think she's still there?"

He nods. "I do. The last image I saw was her being shoved into a lead-lined room."

"Bingo," Calli says, turning and pointing to the stairs leading back up to Brizbin's office. "To the badlands."

The four of us thank our little miner gnome helper and head outside… only to run into Kotah and Hawk coming our way. Kotah's wolf grins at me and then jumps up onto his back legs, shifting as he catches Calli in his arms. "Hello, *Chigua*. How are my girls?"

Calli giggles and rolls her eyes. "Your brother is convinced we're having a girl."

"Because we are," Kotah says, grinning.

"What did you find out?" Hawk asks.

"My sister was taken from here to a heavily guarded compound in the badlands of Travon. We know she's locked in a lead room and is alive, but don't know much more than that."

Hawk shrugs. "That's enough to get us going. Once we get geared up and find ourselves some weapons, we'll be good to go. Does StoneHaven have gun shops?"

Creed shakes his head. "No. After the devastation suffered here, there's a weapon ban in StoneHaven. We'll have to get what we need in Travon."

The van we used earlier to rescue Rhylan rounds the end of

the building and follows the paved driveway to stop not far from where we're gathered. Jaxx parks and he and Brant get out of the front. Then, the back doors open and Rhylan and Dillan get out.

"Oh, he looks much better." As I remark on Rhylan's improved health, Creed strides off to meet him chest-to-chest. Pulling our dragon into his embrace, Creed slaps his back and lets out a long breath. "You look healthy and whole."

Rhylan pulls back and tilts his head. "Thanks to the good doctor."

I draw a deep breath and can't help the shock I know Doc is reading in my expression.

"Uh… yeah," he says, clearing his throat. "Rhylan lost a lot of blood and needed to feed. Things got a little heated…"

I wave away his guilt and move in to hug him. "Don't apologize. Creed's right. Our dragon is healthy and whole and that's what matters."

"What am I missing?" Creed asks, searching our faces. "All I'm getting is anxiety and embarrassment."

I can't imagine a world where I couldn't smell the subtext of life, so I fill him in. "Our mates have gotten to know one another more intimately since we left them. Rhylan's need for blood seems to have forced the issue of bringing us together as mates."

Creed's silver brows arch. "I suppose whatever it takes to get us on the same page works to our favor. We're a bit of a patchwork when it comes to mating."

"But we're getting there," Doc adds.

"One orgasm at a time," Brant says, chuckling.

I roll my eyes. Brant seriously has no filter. Trying to save the boys from further embarrassment, I point to the van. "Back to the problem at hand. We need to get out of here, to the portal hub, find our way to Travon, get weapons, and then rescue Honor."

Kotah blinks. "Oh, is that all?"

Creed

The ten of us pile out of the van in the back lot of the StoneHaven portal hub and make our way toward the main entrance. Before we get far, the buzz of the searing flares hot in my mind, and I buckle, grabbing my head. "Hold up. Something's wrong."

"Keyla? What is it?" The concern in Doc's voice has me twisting to check on my wolf.

She's doubled over too, her eyes gold with the ascension of her wolf. "We can't go in there. I feel it with everything in me. We mustn't go inside."

"Is it your beacon?" Doc asks.

I nod. "Yes, and Keyla's right. It's more than a feeling of foreboding. The energy we're receiving is a definite warning not to enter that building."

"Good enough for me," Calli says. "We've learned to listen to the fae magic mojo. It's never lead us astray."

Rhylan helps me back toward the van and Doc helps Keyla. Once we've retreated and are back where we started, the intensity of the beacon subsides. We straighten and I draw a deep breath. "Let's not trigger a warning like that again."

Keyla chuckles beside me. "Agreed. I think that fried more than a few brain cells."

"Not to belittle your suffering or rush things," Hawk says, frowning as he surveys the land, "but how do we get to Travon now? We need weapons."

"We could fly," Rhy says, looking over the group. "I could carry two and Calli could probably carry two."

Keyla shakes her head. "No. Leaving four people behind when heading into a battle is a bad idea."

"Agreed." I lay my arm across her shoulders and kiss the side of her head. "All of us or none of us."

"No man left behind," Doc says, nodding.

Without portal transportation or flying, I can't see many options. "We'll have to do things the old-fashioned way and drive there. Once we hit the fringe lands, maybe we can find some unsavory characters and bribe them for weapons. Then, we hit the badlands."

Hawk frowns. "What's the currency of the black market here?"

I grunt. "You're asking me? I've never been to the badlands. I have no idea how things are run. Rhy? You're from Travon. Do you know anything about your criminal element in the fringe or badlands?"

"Only by reputation. You know when you're kids and your mother tells you to either stop being a little shit or she'll sell you to one criminal group or another."

Keyla frowns and looks at the others before focusing on Rhylan. "No. My parents were bad but even they didn't do that."

Lukas is frowning now too. "This isn't helping. Do we have access to standard currency here?"

"Quadrant credits," Rhylan says. "Not nearly enough. I've got some savings, but Creed's accounts were frozen the moment Laryssa took over."

"I really hate that woman," Brant grunts.

I bark a laugh. "Back of the line, Bear."

Hawk sighs and looks around. "Does StoneHaven have a ruler?"

Rhylan and I shake our heads. "Not a ruler... but there is a Grand Historian who takes care of the texts."

He shakes his head. "What about a bank? Do you have banks here? Investment firms? Brokerages? Any financial hub will do."

Creed nods. "There's the credit exchange. The finances of the four quadrants are run through them."

"Good enough," Hawk says. "Take me there. I'll see what I can do to get us flush. Surely, with all the things I've seen, the financial backbone of your society can't be all that different from what we're used to."

Lukas gets into the driver's seat and I climb in the front as well. Leaning to the side, I activate the navigation screen in the vehicle while the others climb in the back. When the map on the screen recalibrates and points the way, we get moving.

Hang on, Honor. We're coming little sister.

Doc

As it turns out, Hawk makes quick work of his visit to the credit exchange. The guy knows business and how to talk money with corporate kings. I'm sure it helps that he has more money than the one-percenters and speaks their language.

"Here, I've been assured this should do us." He hands Creed a small briefcase into the back of the van as he climbs in.

Creed opens things up and the guy's ebony eyes grow wide. "Holy fuck, did you just rob the exchange?"

The avian's mouth twitches up in a curt smirk. "No, I leveraged the first contact with the Wolf King of the human realm and took out a personal loan toward establishing a working business relationship."

"Just like that?" Rhylan asks. "And they sent you off with a case full of credits?"

"Well, that and a promise that when we've completed our pressing business, Kotah and I will return with Prince Creed and fill some promises."

Kotah nods to his mate from the other side of the van. "Understood."

Creed nods too. "Whatever it takes. If this gets us Honor, I don't care what you promised them."

Rhylan lets off a soft curse and shakes his head.

I shift to get a better look at the guy and smile. "What's with the huff, Dragon?"

"I keep waiting to see behind the curtain. Are you guys for real? Since when do people put themselves on the line for other people with nothing to gain for themselves?"

Genuine confusion rings in his voice and I feel bad for the guy. "A better question would be why don't the people in your realm care enough about each other to do the same?"

"And it's not for no reason," Hawk says. "We are securing Keyla's future with you and Creed and Doc. It's the right thing to do, helping to free the realm from a usurper queen bitch who has no right to torture the people of this quadrant. And lastly, we're establishing access from the Fae realm to our home and want to make sure the people coming through our portal gate aren't a danger to our world."

Rhy shakes his head. "Sorry, I hear what you're saying—and I believe you mean it—but there's still a part of me waiting for the double-cross."

Brant arches a brow and chuckles. "Quite the skeptic, Dragon."

"You learn what you live."

Keyla offers him a soft smile and reaches over to pat his ankle from where we're sitting on the floor of the van. "Then you need to live a little better. It won't be like that for you, not anymore."

"Where to next?" Lukas asks.

"Wherever it is, let's get there," Brant says. "My ass isn't enjoying the accommodations."

Calli laughs. "That's because Hawk spoils us."

Brant gives his head a shake and smiles. "Maybe. Still, I'm anxious to get to where we're going."

Now it's Jaxx who is laughing. "That's because you smell a fight coming."

He chuckles. "Maybe."

I've known Brant long enough to know there's no maybe about it. My brother bear loves a solid physical confrontation.

"I wish you people had airplanes," Hawk says. "What is going to take us days in this can on wheels would take us hours in my helicopter."

Calli giggles. "What are the odds you can get your Dauphin luxury transport through the gate? It's too big to fit down the halls of the hub stations."

"Wait! That's it!" Creed twists around from the front seat and nods. "We may not be able to use the portal hub station to get to Travon, but the expansion gate might still be an option."

Rhylan's lips turn up in a slow grin. "Yeah, that might work. Although, I don't know that it's ever transported passengers."

Hawk lifts his chin, his gaze expectant. "We're listening. What's an expansion gate?"

Creed starts punching information into the navigation screen on the front dash. "It's exactly that. It's an expanded gate used to transport large items like building materials and conveyances from quadrant to quadrant."

"And there's one here in StoneHaven?"

Creed finishes punching things in and the screen blanks out and starts searching through data. "There would have to be. That's the only way they could've gotten the cranes and building machinery here to rebuild after the wars."

Rhylan nods. "I know for a fact they brought construction cranes here from Travon for the restoration."

"Yes, this area of the realm was destroyed. It took years of restoration to bring it back to what it is today."

When the screen stops cycling through its searches and a

map appears, Creed taps on the closest site. "It's unorthodox for people to use an expanded gate but it's worth a try."

"Well, unorthodox is where we feel most at home," Jaxx says. "Welcome to our world, Dragon."

I chuckle at Rhylan's expression. "True story. Never underestimate how strange things get with the Phoenix Quint as part of the team."

Calli grins. "You're welcome."

~

Keyla

Finding the extended gate site is a little challenging as it's tucked away in an industrial part of the city, but eventually, we find it. Hawk does what Hawk does, and soon enough the ten of us are on our way.

"Your searing beacon isn't weighing in on this at all, is it?" Doc asks.

I take a moment to access the constant buzz in the back of my mind but there's no warning there. Since the moment Creed and I locked gazes, it's been there but usually it's just a little hum I've grown to ignore. "No. Nothing to be alarmed about."

"That's good," Doc says.

"Are you worried about the gate?"

He lifts a muscled shoulder. "Am I the only one who noticed they said no people *ever* use this as a way to get from point A to point B? Why is that? Why wouldn't the foreman go through with his building supplies or a driver stay with his machinery?"

"Are you scared, Bear?" Creed grins, obviously finding his reticence amusing. "I said people *don't* use the expanded gate, not that they *can't* use it. It just doesn't have the same comfort buffers portal gates do."

Calli makes a face. "Does that mean it's going to tingle and burn our skin like our gate does?"

Rhylan nods. "Yeah, but not for so long. These bridges have already been established. It'll be the same feeling but over almost instantly."

That makes me feel better.

Hawk comes out of the foreman's office and points to the briefcase in Creed's hand. "Can I get ten thousand, please?"

Creed frowns. "He's charging for us to go through? Gate portal technology is free. Access is free."

Hawk chuckles. "Not today it isn't. I agreed to one thousand each, and he agreed to look the other way to keep his mouth shut. I think that's credits well spent."

I pat Creed's shoulder and point to the case. "You'll get used to Hawk spending money on us. It's best just to let him do his thing."

Jaxx opens the case and holds it toward Creed. "Our avian likes it when his money paves the way for things he believes in. Don't let it bother you."

Creed sorts through the cards bound in stacks and pulls out ten blue ones with gold trim. "Ten thousand it is," he says, handing them to Hawk. "You got overcharged, but thank you. It means a lot to me that you're willing to help me get my sister back."

Hawk winks. "That's the important part. Money is just money. Family is everything."

I meet Calli's gaze, and the two of us melt a little. Hawk has come so far in the past four months. Being part of the Phoenix Quint has truly brought out the best in him.

Hawk doesn't notice the soft smiles all around him. His focus is solely on paying the foreman and making things happen for us. "All right, that should do it. Ten passengers to portal to Travon. It's been a pleasure, sir."

The foreman smiles at the cards in his hand. "No, sir. The pleasure is mine."

I laugh to myself. *No doubt it is.*

CHAPTER NINETEEN

Rhylan

When we arrive in Travon, I'm flooded with mixed feelings. This quadrant is my home. As kids, Vik and I used to fly with Father to the city and be received like gods. We were the Silverwing dragons.

To be sneaking into the industrial bowels of the city and know I'm not welcome is bad enough. To think that at any moment someone might recognize me, and my shame would infect Creed, Keyla, and Doc is too much.

While Hawk and Lukas speak with the transport master, I keep to the shadows. Slecking hell, I didn't love the idea of coming back here and now I'm downright hating it.

"What's wrong?" Creed lays a hand on my shoulder and turns me to face him. "I sense your turmoil. What's this about?"

Before I answer, Keyla and Dillan join us.

"Are you all right?" Dillan takes my wrist and flips into doctor mode, lifting his watch to start tracking things again.

"I'm fine," I say, reclaiming my arm.

"Pants on fire," Keyla says.

I don't know what she means by that, but see that they aren't buying it.

"Tell us the truth and trust that we want to help you," Keyla says.

For some stupid reason, I want to.

Maybe it's been too long since people genuinely seemed to give a shit about me, or maybe I'm still recovering from being shunned and trying to kill my queen or maybe it's knowing that Vik knows I'm with Creed and chose to send me off with Laryssa rather than warn me what was coming down.

Whatever the reason, these three people are the only thing I have left. After checking that we're alone in our conversation I tell them.

I spill my guts about my family disgrace and my mother being claimed by Shadowcaster, and being sold off to Laryssa as the last-ditch effort to salvage some pride in our brood.

"I'm sorry," I say, rubbing the ache in my chest. "When I claimed Creed, I never thought about how my garbage life would reflect on you. Slecking hell, you're the royal couple of Dornte and I'm the sludge on the bottom of your shoe."

"Well, that's dramatic," Calli says, blinking. "How about you let us decide what we should be protected from? What happened to you was unfair. You don't have to bow to your brood alpha to get the approval and respect you deserve. You're mated to the royal couple of Dornte. You're the shit now, baby."

Keyla chuckles. "That's her way of saying you don't need them, you have us."

"That's what I said," Calli says, chuckling.

"And as for being recognized and exposing us to the bad stink of your family drama," Doc says. "Bring it on. Your brood has never seen family drama like we've got backing us up."

"True story," Calli says, joining us. "Sometimes found family is a shit ton more powerful than blood family. When you grow

up without the connections you need, you're extra protective of them when you find them and make them with others."

"Well said, kitten," Jaxx says as he and the others join us. "The best revenge will be for you to show your alpha and your brood that they were holding you back."

Keyla grins. "You're better off without them."

Kotah nods. "And, when we end Laryssa's claim on the throne, you'll be mated to the king and queen of the quadrant."

"And let us tell you from experience," Brant says grinning. "That's a sweet place to be."

I pan my gaze across the warm expressions of the group, who up until this week, were strangers living in another realm.

Can this really be happening?

Can these people be meant to be my refuge?

Yes, they can, Creed says directly into my mind. *They are the real deal. It's crazy and it took a few days for me to wrap my head around it too, but this is our future, Rhy. From now on, it's the four of us with the quint at our backs.*

What about Vik? What do I say to him? How do I explain any of this to my twin?

I can't tell you that. All I know is you're right where you need to be. Accept it. Embrace it. And when the dust settles, we'll figure out a way to make it right with your brother... and we'll be there for you no matter how that turns out.

Creed sweeps his hand through my hair and brushes the flop of my bangs back to look me in the eyes. *Let them see you, Rhy. I promise you won't regret it.*

The meaning behind Creed's words is poignant. For so long, with my brood mates watching and judging, I've put on this hard ass persona to keep up the front.

Self-loathing is like a virus.

When there is an outbreak, it festers and spreads, consuming all the good and healthy things in its path.

I'm tired, Creed. I'm really slecking tired.

Then let us share your burden and we'll do the same. I truly believe that's why the universe stepped in. We're supposed to come together and do what none of us could manage alone.

Pulling up the hood of the sweatshirt Doc loaned me, I tuck my hair back and out of my face. I feel more than a little exposed, but I suppose that's the point. I'm letting them see me.

Creed's mental caress means I'm on the right track and then Keyla moves in and presses a gentle hand on my cheek. "It's nice to have you with us, Rhy. It might not feel like it at first, but if there's something we've all learned this week, it's that after the shockwaves subside, we're better for the explosion of our lives."

I think about Vikarus and Shadowcaster and everything that happened with the queen. Then I think about Sebastian White-house Senior, Hunter, and how their person poisoned Keyla's father to put Kotah into office.

Yeah, explosion is about right.

~

Creed

When Hawk and Lukas are finished with the transport master, they walk us over to where a fleet of trucks and shuttles are lined up for rent. "I opted for two large SUVs over one shuttle," Hawk says. "That way, if we run into trouble, we've got twice as many options."

"Trouble?" Calli says. "Why on earth would you be expecting trouble?"

They find that amusing and I can only imagine what they faced during Calli's quest to open the portal rift.

It doesn't take long for us to divvy up and get into our vehicles. It's the four of us in our truck and the Phoenix Quint and Lukas in the other.

"Rhy?" I tap the nav screen on the rental and wake it for

input. "Any ideas where to start looking for weapons suppliers in the fringe lands?"

He nods. "Take the Mark Six Trail north toward Granite Ridge. There's a traveling swap meet where you can get anything and everything for the right price."

I punch in the information and lower the window to lean out and tell Lukas our destination. "Follow close. Two nice trucks driving in the fringe are going to draw attention. Be ready for anything."

"How long do we have before we need to be on guard?" Jaxx asks, from the back seat.

"A little under two hours based on what the destination information says on my screen."

Lukas rolls his eyes. "Seriously, Jaguar. Keep it in your pants."

"You just keep your eyes on the road, soldier man. Don't you worry about what's goin' on in the back."

I roll my window up and look at Doc and Keyla in the mirror behind me. "Is Jaxx really going to start something up while we're driving into the fringe or is he messing with the guy?"

Keyla snorts. "Oh, he's probably already naked."

"With Lukas in the truck?"

"What do you think I've been trying to tell you? They're insatiable and have no threshold for modesty or propriety."

"At least he warned Lukas to keep eyes front," Doc says, chuckling. "We could've used a few of those warnings over the past four months."

Rhylan chuckles. "Well, I suppose that's one way to pass the travel time."

"Sleeping is another," Keyla says, lying down across the seat and resting her head in Dillan's lap. "It's been a long, emotional day. I'm going to close my eyes for a little bit."

Doc gets her all cozied in and brushes her hair back with

such a look of adoration in his gaze it feels too intimate to watch... and yet, I do. Watching the two of them loving each other fills my heart with hope.

One day soon, 'love' might be a word we all can share. And as wonderful as it's been so far, I'm looking forward to that.

∾

Keyla

I wake sometime later and the world is in darkness. I'm still lying on the seat of the truck but Doc is gone and the only other scent in the vehicle with me is Rhylan. His breathing is slow and steady in the seat behind me, but his scent says he's anxious.

Shifting up to sit, I stretch and look around. "Where are we?"

"We're in the Travon fringe in Granite Ridge. Hawk and Lukas are in negotiating weapons for us. Doc and Creed are stretching their legs and taking a piss."

"And you got stuck babysitting?"

"Mostly they want me to stay out of sight."

"Would people here recognize you? Is your brood from the fringe?"

"Not from around here, but yes, my brother and I are recognized often. The Silverwing twins carry a bit of celebrity. Our family is well known in Travon."

I hear the sadness in his voice and smell the acrid bitterness of his scent. "I'm sorry life turned on you."

"It is what it is."

As crappy as things got for Kotah and me at times, we never lost our place in society. Sometimes we wished we weren't royals but after seeing the damage done to Rhylan and Vikarus, I'm glad we didn't get our wish.

"Well, you're in good company. In this mating and this

family, what happened before means nothing. The only thing we're interested in is moving forward as a solid unit."

With that in mind, I push up on my knees and lean over the seat to kiss his cheek.

Rhylan recoils and shifts to the other end of the back seat. "Uh... sorry. I don't think you want to do that, Princess."

I frown. "Kiss your cheek? It's hardly scandalous. We're mated to the same man and one day soon, I'm hoping the four of us will be a united quadruple."

He swallows and shakes his head. "I think we should just be friends and allies."

"Friends? I think the chemistry between us is already beyond friendship."

"How about friends with sexual tension?"

"Why do you want that?" I chuckle. Then it hits me. Him turning down those women the other night. Backing away and trying to get that girl out of his pants. "Oh... are you gay?"

"*What?* No. How'd you get there?"

I climb over the seat so there are no barriers between us. "Maybe that's the real reason you were turning down those girls in your suite the other night. If that's the case, you can tell me. I meant what I said. You're safe with us, no matter what."

Reaching forward, he shifts on the seat and pulls me to straddle his lap. His hands squeeze my hips before running a hot trail of tingles as he strokes a line up my sides from my hip to the swell of my breasts. Taking a detour inland, he finds the tightened nipples pushing against the fabric of my shirt and captures them between his fingers and thumbs.

The gentle tweak of him squeezing sends a rush of damp heat to my core and his body responds with a blast of arousal.

I suck in a breath. "So, not gay then."

"Definitely not gay."

As much as I want to lean in and start something hot and wet with him, I ease back and rein in my wild side. "Then why

do you want to keep it friends between us? It seems you had no objections moving forward with Doc."

"I had a lot of objections but needed to feed."

"But the two of you seem good now."

He nods. "Yeah, Doc's cool."

"He's also great with his mouth."

The flash of light in his eyes is playful and sweet. "I found that out."

"So, you claim Creed as your own and you enjoyed getting to know Doc sexually. Why am I the exception?"

"I just think... I don't want you to find out things and think I took advantage. There are things I need to talk to you about. Things you need to know but I wanted to talk to Creed first."

"If they are things I need to know, why speak to Creed first?"

"Because I barely know you. I'm not sure how to talk to you or how you'll welcome what I've got to say."

I take his hands in mine and offer him an open smile. "You said there are things I need to know, so just tell me."

He swallows and shakes his head. "I think I should wait and talk to Creed first. You're his female and I don't want to ruin things."

"I'm bound to three males, yourself included. As you get to know me, you'll find out what I hate most is being treated like a royal flower. I'm not that girl. If you've got something to say to me, *say it*." My words come out harsher than I intend but his rising anxiety is upsetting my wolf.

I release his hands and grip the front of his shirt. I'm still straddling his lap and for some reason, I feel like I'll need to hang on for this.

We lock gazes and Rhylan swallows. "Your father was poisoned to put your brother in power. Sebastian and Laryssa believed the instability of having an ostracized boy prince taking over the realm would leave an opening for Hawk's father to assume command of your realm. Then, when he was king,

Laryssa would have a foothold in the criminal activities that were making him so wealthy and powerful. They had an alliance and were close to completing it when the universe put the prophecy into motion."

I hear his words and while it sounds like something from an espionage novel and not my life, I smell the truth of his words. "There was speculation... The cook at the palace said she believed Father was being poisoned, but no one believed her."

"From what I know, they moved slowly to ensure no one grew suspicious. It took years to get it done."

Hot tears warm my cheeks as I think of the senseless loss. "He wasn't a great father but he was an incredible king. He and my mother ruled together and no one questioned the course of the realm."

"I'm sorry, Princess. Things were set in motion long before Laryssa stole Creed's throne. I only learned about the steps Laryssa had taken in bits and pieces over the past two years, but Sebastian's agent in the palace had been there for a decade or more."

"Who was it? Do you know?"

"The royal liaison. It was a woman who acted as their assistant."

"Raven." The name tastes sour on my tongue. "Kotah came to me with the possibility and I threw it back at him. Raven was my friend and there was no way I would listen to such lies about her."

Climbing off Rhylan's lap, I flop on the bench seat beside him. "Maybe if I had listened Father might've been saved."

"Nothing good comes from second-guessing what is done," he says. "Trust me. Vik and I tried for years to figure out if life would've been different if our father hadn't stood his ground to keep our mother. What if he left and didn't fight? What if he shared her? What if he'd been strong enough to win? The 'what if' game takes you around in circles but changes nothing."

I swipe my face with the sleeve of my shirt. "Don't tell Kotah."

"What? Why? I thought you two would want to know and maybe act on it."

I push my grief down and get my head back on track. "Kotah never wanted to be king. He stepped up because he was forced to and is in a good place right now. With the help of Calli, Hawk, and the others, he'll do well. There's less than a decade left on the wildling reign anyway. There's no need for him to know our father was killed because he was expected to fail."

"All right. It's your story to tell. If you want to keep it between us, I'm fine with that."

I draw a steadying breath and reach forward to take his hand. "What I want to know now is why you thought this would affect how I feel about you?"

"It doesn't?"

"Did you plot to have my father killed?"

"No, but I was present during Laryssa's discussions at Stone-Haven. I heard the messages from Hawk's father. I made no attempt to help him or persuade her to not go along with her plans."

I squeeze his hand. "You give yourself too much credit. If there's one thing I know—it's political ambition. There's nothing a dragon bodyguard could do or say to derail people like Laryssa and Sebastian. I don't hold you responsible in any way."

The doors to the truck open and Creed and Doc climb in. Doc hasn't even sat on his seat before his bear is rumbling off a violent growl. "What did you do, Dragon? Why has she been crying?"

Creed cranks around from the front seat and frowns. "What's going on, Little Wolf? Are you all right?"

I raise a hand to stop the onslaught. "I'm fine. Rhylan informed me of a few things Laryssa was involved in that

affected Kotah and me. My grief is for my father, not myself. It seems she and Sebastian had him killed as part of their plan to destabilize our realm and take control."

"Oh, babe, I'm sorry," Doc says, flopping on the seat in front of us and reaching over. "So, Adahy was right about the poisoning?"

I nod, tears stinging my eyes once again. "About all of it. Rhy says Sebastian's person on the inside is the royal liaison."

"Raven. Damn, that's hard to believe. She always seems so committed to your family."

"I don't want Kotah to know yet. I want to think about how to tell him, so he doesn't take it personally."

"Well, he can't have her on his staff. He'll have to be told something."

I run my hand over my forehead and sigh. "I know. I'll speak with Hawk privately and discuss it with him. He'll know best how to deal with something like this."

Rhylan's mouth quirks up at the side. "You guys give Hawk a lot of credit on things. I thought him taking charge of everything was because he's an autocratic alpha but you respect the guy."

Dillan and I both nod. "He's earned that respect a hundred times over in the past months. As you get to know him, you'll realize he's as powerful strategically and intellectually as he is in a corporate setting."

"True story," Doc says. "People see wealthy arrogance, but he's much more than that."

"I hate to rush this," Creed says, still staring back from the front of the truck. "The quint is ready to roll. Are we good?"

I nod. "Yeah. Let's go find your sister."

CHAPTER TWENTY

Creed

Thanks to the visions Honor left for me in the embedding of her traveler bed, I have a strong sense of where we're going. If the queen's guards had blindfolded her or covered her head, I wouldn't be able to track her whereabouts with such certainty.

As it is, I follow her memories and watch for the road signs and landscape markers she took note of so I could track her.

"The address for the factory that supplied the lead panels corresponds to this area." Rhylan has the back seat reading light on and is going through the folders with Doc. "I have a good feeling about this."

I'm glad.

I need all the good feelings I can get because if Laryssa knows we attacked a compound where she had Honor and we don't find her there, she'll move her somewhere new and make her suffer for my insolence.

"What about your demon wolf?" Keyla asks from the seat beside me. "You mentioned you think the witch and likely the queen can track you when you're in your cursed form. Do you think they're able to track you if you haven't shifted?"

"I don't think so." I hit my indicator and ease off the paved road to head across the dirt tracks of rough terrain. "I avoid shifting into that beast because it steals a bit of my soul every time I do. Something about the magic behind the curse makes me feel less myself with every change. I don't think they can access the beast if it isn't activated. Rhy? Do you know anything about that?"

"Not officially," Rhy says, "but I don't think they can track you as a man because the times you disappeared, Laryssa was beside herself screaming at us to find you before you disabled the tracker in your back. If she could track you by the curse, I don't think she would've been so crazy."

I didn't think so either, but it's nice to hear. After ten minutes of driving straight out into the middle of nowhere, we come to an old, broken sign for what used to be the town of Magic Springs. "Population forty-four thousand," I say, reading the chipped paint.

Keyla leans forward and frowns out the front windshield. "I'd be surprised if there is a population of forty-four people out here now."

"This is what the badlands are about, Little Wolf. Only the worst off and those who can no longer blend with civilization remain here."

"The perfect place to hold up and not be found."

I draw a deep breath. "Only, we are here and we've found them."

"And once we have your sister and the two of you get a chance to regroup, we'll put our heads together to figure out how to reclaim your quadrant."

"I love how you and your family speak about reclaiming my throne as a certainty. *When* we reclaim your throne... *when* we beat Laryssa… *when* we find the blood witch and break her curse. I've never known such optimism."

Keyla smiles over at me from her seat and the light from the second moon casts her face into silver light. "My father always used to say, *'A leader must embrace his duty—despite personal sentiment, obstacles, dangers, or pressures from others. To fail in this is to lose the honor of being a male of worth.'* He made Kotah and I memorize that and repeat it to him all the time."

I hear the sadness in her voice and reach over to take her hand in mine. "I'm sorry about your father. It sickens me that he lost his life in a plot he'll never know he was targeted in. It's not right. A male should be able to face his foes."

She forces a smile. "Agreed. Poisoning him and sneaking around in the shadows of your castle, pitting civilians against royal families… it just proves how weak and cowardly Laryssa and Sebastian are."

"Thankfully, that's a moot point where Hawk's father is concerned," Doc says.

"Yeah. Still, I want to get back to our realm and get Raven away from my mother."

I pull off the main road leading into the eerie and desolate town and turn off my lights as we roll quietly down the back lane toward the last leg of the compound. It's on the outskirts of nowhere and when we get close enough, I pull off the road. Finding some bushes, I tuck the truck out of sight and Lukas follows with his vehicle.

"Rhy, grab some branches and see if you can conceal the truck as much as possible.

"I'll help," Doc says.

As they jump out, it's easy to see a relationship is building between those two. "It seems like we might have ourselves a functional foursome in the works after all. Honestly, two days ago, I never would have thought it possible."

Keyla's grin lights up her beautiful face. "I'm glad. I didn't want you to forfeit someone you obviously cared for simply for the propriety of what your realm is accustomed to."

"I'm not sure how you knew I cared for him. I didn't realize it until all this crashed around us."

She chuckles. "Call it women's intuition. We're a powerful force, you know."

"Oh, I know. Growing up watching Honor train to be the Queen of the Amberloq taught me that. Even before her powers transferred, she was a force."

"It'll be interesting to see what happens next. I understand the Amberloq lost their leader when your aunt was killed, but what I want to know is where they went and why they haven't tried to rescue Honor?"

"The Amberloq forces were decimated in the Wars of Power. By the time Laryssa launched her plans against my family, the ancient sect was already lost."

"Making it that much easier to seize your quadrant."

"It was a large part of her success, yes. And I'm sure it didn't help that with the estrangement of my father and his sister, Valorous didn't live in or near the castle. How can the Guardian of the Throne protect the throne if she's in another part of the quadrant?"

Keyla sighs. "I'm sorry the fallout of their troubles allowed Laryssa to sweep in and take control."

"My parents and my aunt lost their lives because of their inability to work together. I'll never allow that to happen with Honor."

"And you shouldn't. Kotah and I don't always agree but there is nothing I wouldn't do for him and him for me. I have never doubted that."

Even in the short time I've known the two of them, I've seen that. "I know Honor and deeply respect her inner strength. If anyone can bring the ancient order of her guardians back from the brink of extinction, it's her."

Keyla straightens. "Then we need to get her back and set her free to do her thing."

~

Doc

Lukas, Hawk, Rhylan, and I go through some of the tactical gear we were able to acquire at the black-market swap meet back in the fringe lands. The weapons are weird, powered by pulse cartridges, and are more sci-fi than I'm comfortable with. The night vision goggles, flak vests, and drones are cool and of good quality.

Rhylan takes control of the drone as soon as we're in position, and fifteen minutes later, he's downloading data and pulling up a schematic of the property on a data pad. When he's ready, he sets it on the front hood of Hawk's truck.

"That's fine work, Dragon," Hawk says, grinning.

Rhy shrugs. "The drone did the work. I just transferred the data."

"So, what have we got?" Creed asks.

"The compound is a large gated rectangle with a sentry guard on each corner. There are three main buildings and four outbuildings. Honor could be held in any of them."

Lukas frowns. "We'll need to hit the sentries in a coordinated strike. We've only got two sniper rifles, so two people will have to scale the towers and eliminate their targets face-to-face and as quietly as possible."

"I'll take one," Hawk says. "I can fly up and shift as I descend. Not an issue."

"I'll take the other," Jaxx says. "Those towers are made of

wood. My jaguar can scale twenty feet in two seconds and then shift and take mine out before he knows what hit him."

Lukas nods. "That leaves Doc and me with the sniper rifles."

I nod. "Okay, so the sentries are down, what then?"

Hawk points toward the lit-up map. "Once the sentries are down, I want Calli in the northeast tower and Rhylan in the southwest. You two are our offensive line. You'll watch our backs and radio us if there's trouble. Otherwise, we need to keep this as quiet as possible."

"The other eight of us will search the compound in two teams of four. Kotah and Keyla will take point as wolves and try to scent Honor and track her down. The other three in each team will keep them safe."

Creed frowns. "You want Keyla to take point in an offensive assault? I'm not comfortable with that."

Hawk turns a sympathetic gaze to the guy and nods. "I understand your need to protect your mate, but honestly, even before Lukas, Doc, and I began training the ladies for battle, Keyla was a proficient fighter. She's had hand-to-hand and weapons mastery training her entire life. You haven't seen her in action yet, but she's as much of a force out there as you or me."

Creed passes an assessing gaze over our girl and she doesn't seem to mind.

"He's right, my prince. And after the past four months battling with Calli and the boys, I'm in the best conditioning I've ever been in. Don't let the princess thing fool you."

The prince looks at me and I give him a reassuring nod. "S'all good. And we'll be there to back her up."

When he relents, we spend a few more minutes going over the map of the compound, and then it's time to gear up and get ready to roll out.

I spend that time assessing the workings of the sniper rifle and get a sense of the settings. Thankfully, it's not that different from the guns I used in the military. Lukas and I take the weapons aside and crack off a few practice shots to get a feel for the trigger and the accuracy. Then we're good to go.

"Good luck, babe," I say, leaning in for a kiss. "Be safe. I'll take my shot and get down to you as quickly as I can."

"Right and tight," Keyla says. "Don't rush. Be safe."

"Take care of our girl until I get there," I say to Creed and Rhy.

The quint says their private goodbyes and then Hawk checks his FCO watch and makes sure we all have ours on. "We take out the sentries in ten minutes on my mark. Ready... Mark."

I set the countdown, kiss Keyla once more, and then knuckle bump Rhylan and Creed. "Don't get dead boys. We can only be a quadruple with all four of us, so no casualties."

Everyone nods and dissolves into the darkness.

~

Keyla

Creed, Rhylan, and I wait as Doc sets up his shot from a vantage point in the trees that border the compound. I don't have the countdown, so there's nothing to do but wait silently in the darkness.

You're nervous. Creed slides his marked palm against mine and tugs me against his chest. My body melts against his willingly and I press my cheek against the solid plane of his chest. *Dillan's a military man, isn't he? He can make this shot.*

I don't doubt his skill with weapons in our realm, but your space blasters are different.

Not that different, Rhylan says. *He'll be fine. Once the sentries are taken out, Hawk will fly down and open the gate. I'll take Doc's weapon and cover your entry from above. Quick and quiet.*

I offer Rhy a smile and wish we were closer.

I'd like to hug him and tell him to be careful but don't want to push the situation. It was only half an hour ago when he said he didn't want to move forward with me romantically. I think that was only because of his knowledge of what happened to my father, but we haven't had a chance to revisit that yet.

The soft *pffft* sound in the branches above wouldn't be audible by a human but my wolf is close to the surface and my senses are heightened for the situation.

Rhylan and I both look up to where Doc is barely visible among the foliage of the tree. He flashes me a thumbs up and my heart beats a little easier.

"The sentries are down. It's go time." Reaching up, I kiss Creed and cup his chiseled jaw. "Be safe."

"You too, Little Wolf. Recovering Honor has no meaning if I lose you in the process." He growls into my mouth as we come together in one last loving kiss. We have grown confident with one another over the past week—confident and passionate.

We both need for this to work out.

We both need to see where this adventure takes us.

Ending the kiss, I brush my lips over his again, breathing him deep into my soul. "Everything will be fine. We're destined for great things."

Easing back I abandon my original plan to play it cool with Rhylan and hug him. "Be safe, Dragon. You and I have a lot of getting to know one another to do and I'm looking forward to it."

I catch the surprise in his expression as I lace my fingers into his hair. Closing the distance between us, I pull his mouth down to mine. Whatever this is, the searing, the plus-ones, the need to belong, we are bound to one another and I need him to know I genuinely care about his well-being.

Where the kiss with Creed was laced with emotion and worry, Rhylan's is tentative and stiff... at first. Then, I let my wolf ascend further to call his wildling side. His dragon follows the primal call, deepening the connection as his tongue sweeps the seam of my lips and invades.

I swallow and step back. "A promise for later."

My words come out a little breathless but I'm not the only one whose chest is pumping.

This is what it could be like. We could have it all.

"Move out." Doc drops from the tree, hands Rhylan the gun, and smacks his shoulder. "Be safe, Dragon. And hey, if you need to feed later, consider my veins an open invitation."

Rhylan chuckles. "I'll keep that in mind."

And with that, I launch forward and invite my wolf to rise to the fore. Shifting on the fly is the work of a thought. A wildling's transformation is based within magic, not biology.

It's painless, quick, and a joy to embrace.

When we arrive at the gate, Calli is there with Kotah, Brant, and Lukas. My brother and Brant are in their wildling forms as are Doc and I.

In the dark of night, Kotah's coat looks black as he brushes his shoulder against mine. He licks the side of my muzzle and lets off a soft whine. The guttural sound is his wolf's way of telling me to be careful.

I nip at the fur covering his cheek and lick him back.

The soft slide of steel bolts shifting in their tracks precedes Hawk opening the gate. He doesn't say a word, just pats my shoulder and Kotah's as we lead our pack inside.

I have a bit of an advantage because when Creed showed me around the royal suite, he also showed me Honor's bedroom. His sister has a distinct scent... well, everyone does, but hers is memorable.

It's like summer rain and stubborn strength.

I take the right wall and Kotah and his posse take the left. My thinking is that if we start at the garage or where the vehicle that brought her parked, I might be able to pick up a trace of her scent and follow it.

It's been weeks—closer to a month—since Riley last contacted Calli, so if that was when she was captured at Stone-Haven and brought here, it was long enough ago that the scent will be faint and diluted at best.

CHAPTER TWENTY-ONE

Creed

S ticking to the shadows, Doc, Lukas, and I follow my white wolf. She's breathtaking in her wolf form: lithe and graceful, muscled and deadly. And although they assured me she can take care of herself, I still worry.

After everything life has taken from me, I won't lose my other half. She is mine and no one and nothing is worth losing her.

Not even my sister.

Glancing up at the southwest tower, I search for any sign of Rhylan. Hawk is smart to have him and Calli as our sentries. From their perches, they can be airborne at a moment's notice, they can cover any incoming threats, and they can cut off runners who might escape our net.

Keyla says he's a strategic power.

I hope that ensures our success.

Keyla's footing slows and she lifts her nose off the ground. Rising onto her back paws, she sniffs the perimeter wall. *I've got her scent here. It's faint, but it's her.*

Maybe they pushed her up against the wall when they were bringing her in?

Yeah, maybe.

It still baffles me that Keyla can open her own channels of communication. It's like she's absorbed my power and took it on as her own.

She truly is amazing.

Dropping back to all fours, she continues. She bypasses the first two outbuildings, which look to be a tool shed and a bunkhouse. Lukas and I bend to duck below the windows as we progress. It's close to three in the morning, so hopefully, other than the sentries, everyone else is tucked in and fast asleep.

When we get to what looks like a small, guesthouse, Keyla sniffs along the threshold of the door and then looks at Lukas. *Her scent goes inside.*

I whisper Keyla's words to Lukas and the man moves forward. He's dark-haired and has the same military frame as Dillan but he carries magical energy that makes my gift tingle.

He's powerful, but nobody looking at him from across the room or talking to him would know just how lethal he could be.

Which makes him more powerful by my estimation.

Lukas places a hand over the latch plate of the door and a surge of power snaps in the air. After drawing his weapon, he lowers his goggles and readies for the infiltration. The door makes no sound as it's opened an inch. He checks things aren't rigged to catch intruders unaware, and then leads the way in.

True to what it looked like from the outside, it's a guesthouse. And it's empty.

It only takes Lukas and me a moment to search the two bedrooms and one bath. Nothing in the closets. No one here at all.

I'm disappointed.

Keyla seemed so sure.

A soft whine brings my attention to my girl sitting on the floor. When she has my attention, she paws at the floor beside the sofa. *Her scent is coming up from between the floorboards.*

I holster my weapon, and gesture for Lukas to help me move the furniture. The two of us shift things out of the way and flip the carpet back.

Nicely done, Little Wolf.

Lukas kneels beside the metal door hatch and places his hand on the locking mechanism. A moment later, he opens things up and reveals the rungs of a ladder.

Looking back, he points to Doc and then the door. Then he points to Keyla and the open door. She sniffs at the opening and her wolf drops into the darkness without question.

My heart kicks up a fuss. I certainly wouldn't send her down first. What the fuck?

Annoyed, I drop to the floor, swing my feet down, and grab the rungs. *Keyla? Are you all right?*

Fine. Come. I think I've found the lead vault.

It's pitch black down here and for a moment I think about using the night vision of my cursed self. But no. If there's any chance that could notify Laryssa or the blood witch that we're moving in, I'd rather go blindly into the dark. Pulling down the goggles Hawk and Lukas picked up while we were in the fringe, I give my eyes a moment to adjust.

The brush of Keyla's wolf against my thigh is comforting. *Hey, sexy girl. Show me what you've found.*

My heart is racing as we jog down the dirt tunnel. Obviously, this pathway goes beneath the compound and not just under the guesthouse because, after fifty feet, we're still moving.

A quick glance behind us assures me that Lukas is on our heels and backing us up. Good. He's much more than a great door opener but having him open the doors is awesome.

Here. Keyla paws at the wall. *I smell her in here.*

I don't see anything. In fact, the wall shows no sign of even having a break for a door.

"It's a glamor," Lukas whispers beside me. "Give me some room and I'll see what I can do about taking it out of play."

Keyla and I step back, and I run my fingers through her long, silky coat while we wait. Touching her has quickly become my foundation in life.

From that first night locked in that cabin while we tried to figure out what our searing meant, to this moment now, the one constant has been that having her close not only eases me but strengthens me.

I love you, Little Wolf. I'm so, incredibly thankful you're the other half of my soul. Where I am the dark and damaged, you are the light.

Keyla shifts and rises before me, reaching her arms around my neck. She's naked and her skin is hot and cock-achingly soft. *I love you too. When this is over... when our time and privacy is our own... I want you to meet me back in my grotto for some fun in the sun. I want time with us as a group too, but I need some alone time with you.*

Agreed. I can't wait.

The deep-throated male chuckle across the hall brings our attention back to Lukas smiling at us.

"Love is in the air," Keyla says, flashing clothes on.

"And it's highly contagious. I don't think there's been a day in four months that I haven't caught someone naked and getting frisky."

Keyla giggles. "Like Calli says. We need to find you someone awesome enough to deserve you."

He winks and then tilts his head toward what is now visibly a lead door. "How about we finish the extraction first and worry about my lack of a love life later."

"Deal. Let's do this."

~

Doc

They've been down there a really long time. My bear is wearing a path in the floorboards as I check the front windows, round the sofa, listen at the trap door in the floor, and then complete the circuit back around to the front windows.

Silence isn't necessarily a bad thing.

It could be a good thing—a great thing. Maybe they've found Creed's sister, hit no snags, and are about to pop up out of the floor.

Maybe...

Any minute now...

My bear lets off a soft grunt of frustration and I go for another round. I plod toward the door when it swings open and I'm suddenly looking at two very surprised men in battle fatigues.

Before they get their weapons up, I charge and bat their guns out of play. Head down, I barrel through them, forcing them outside. The crashing of bodies and bear breaks the silence of the night and I curse.

If men are sleeping in the barracks next door, they are definitely awake.

The two men who found us scramble to their feet and separate enough that I can't keep them both in my sights at once.

I focus on the one about to reach his weapon and end that big idea once and for all. Stomping on the silver blaster, I crush the possibility of it ever firing again.

I turn and am about to race back toward the other one when the door to the barracks opens and bad guy reinforcements start hemorrhaging out of the building like clowns out of a Volkswagen.

Shit. Shit. Shit.

I crank my head around to assess my chances of making it back inside the guesthouse, but I'm cut off. Head down, I dig my mighty claws into the earth and charge the incoming hostiles. If nothing else, I can bowl a few over and cause a panic.

Annoyingly, it's these moments I wish I was as big and intimidating as Brant. That asshole's grizzly is something to be truly feared. I've actually seen grown men wet their pants when he's charging them.

Still, my black bear is not to be dismissed.

Digging in, I ready for things to go south. There's no way I can fend off ten or twelve men and come out the victor.

Damn. This is going to suck.

Rhylan

I hear the commotion a moment before I see a black bear charging a crowd of men exiting the long outbuilding along the opposite wall. The guy is seriously outmanned.

On a running leap, I launch over the rail of the tower and burst into my dragon. With a couple of pumps of my wings, I build up enough speed to dive into the mix and do some real damage.

Zooming in unseen, I extend my talons and start picking off the men trying to kill my bear.

I laugh at myself as I rise back into the air, crunch the two men I have clutched in my grip, and arc back around for another go.

When did he become *my* bear?

I think that was at some point when I was swallowing his blood and he was sucking my dick so good I thought I might pass out.

If signing up for this quadruple thing means I can get that on the regular, I'm game to give it a try.

At the height of my turn, I drop the two I had and go in for

JL MADORE

two more. On the way down, I catch the headlights of three vehicles coming up the road.

Who invited friends?

This is supposed to be a private party.

The hiss and zing of laser fire below have me torn between cutting off the incoming troops and helping Doc with his outmanned situation.

The night sky bursts into flame as Calli reads my mind. Her phoenix launches off the platform of the far tower and she spews a line of fire to cut off the incoming caravan.

With that taken care of, I return my attention to the fight in progress. This time, when I drop from the sky, I see the stunning white wolf rushing the cluster of men.

I follow her path back to find Creed carrying the limp body of his sister. Her silver hair is twice as long as Creed's but there's no mistaking her.

We did it. We found Honor.

For the first time in a very long time, I feel like I'm on the right side of a battle. I knew working for Laryssa was crushing my soul but at this moment it's so evident I wonder how I lasted as long as I did.

Arcing in the night sky, I head back to my mates.

It's crazy, but I'm actually starting to think of them like that. Creed worked his way under my skin long ago but the other two are just as infectious.

Pulling back on my wings, I use reverse thrust to hover above Creed as he makes for the gate. Calli has the new arrivals blocked off well enough that he, Lukas, and Keyla can get her out of the compound and start heading for our trucks hidden down the road.

Hawk meets them at the gate and he must speak to his mates telepathically because they all start to pull out. I circle the compound to give cover to the two bears, the chocolate wolf, and the jaguar tearing people to shreds.

206

Not that they need my help.

These guys are wicked lethal.

The shrill shriek of Calli's phoenix has my gaze pivoting just in time to brace for impact. The mid-air collision is hard and fast and takes me toppling through the open night sky. Pushing off, I curse and crack my attacker with the spine of my wing.

With a grunt, my brother is thrown back and I have the necessary space to land a half-mile up the road. Shifting as I approach the ground, I'm ready for the tackle as Vikarus does the same.

Fists flying the two of us go down.

"What's your problem, asshole," I shout, grappling for a solid hold as we roll in the dirt. "I'd think you'd be glad to see I'm not dead."

"My brother *is* dead," he spits, rolling over me.

I catch the backswing of his arm right before his fist connects with my jaw and nearly spins my head around on my neck.

"I don't know what that silver-haired freak did to mess up your mind, but you're not my brother."

The venom in his words sends a shaft of icy poison straight to my heart. "Creed didn't do anything, and you know it. He only got his powers back this week. I've been with him for years."

"Liar!" Vik shouts. "My brother was a great soldier with unquestionable honor. He wouldn't do the things they said you did."

"What did I do?" I snap, evading a punch. "Aside from where my cock was at night, what did I do? I followed orders. I did the queen's bidding. I never once failed to fulfill my duty… and what did that get me? She ordered me dead in her car and had me shot three times at close range."

"Of course, she did. You ripped off her slecking hand."

I swipe at the sweat on my brow and shake my head. "You've

been given an edited version of what happened. I was shot and bleeding out when I grabbed her briefcase and made a run for it. I didn't even know about her hand until they rescued me."

Vik's gaze narrows on me but he can smell that I'm telling him the truth.

"Yes, I fell for Creed, and that was unprofessional, but I carried out all my duties for Laryssa and I would've continued to do so if I hadn't almost died as a reward for my loyalty."

He shakes his head. "You don't look like you almost died. You look like you're fairing pretty slecking well with your boyfriend and his new crew."

"Doc healed me with Calli's tears and fed me. I'm strong because they rescued me."

"They *turned* you."

I curse and swipe my hair out of my eyes. "No, Vik. Have you listened to anything I've been telling you this week. We were on the wrong side. The magic of the fae universe resurrected the phoenix to stop Laryssa and Whitehouse from securing the rift and taking over the crown of the other realm. It acted again by soul-searing Keyla and Creed together and restoring his powers and a way for him to regain his quadrant. The very world we live to protect is telling us what needs to happen and you refuse to see it."

"I'm trying to save our family name, our reputation, and our mother's honor."

"This is bigger than us, Vik! This is more important than what Shadowcaster and the brood think of us. This is about the future of the realm."

Vik shakes his head. "My brother... my *real* brother would know that *nothing* is more important than our family honor."

"I do know that, my brother. It's just you think we regain our family honor by pleasing Laryssa and Shadowcaster. It's not. We restore our honor by doing what's right at any cost. It's about living true to our core beliefs and fighting for what we believe in."

Vik shakes his head. "You're wrong."

"I don't think so."

The two of us stand there a long time, stuck in a deadlock of wills. I hear the shouts and fighting back at the compound and everything in me wants to be back there helping my newfound family but keeping my blood family busy so he doesn't interfere is important to their success.

"Trust me, Vik. Come with me and get to know them. Think about what I'm saying. You'll see I'm right. Creed is meant to reclaim the quadrant. We can be on the right side of this. It's not too late."

Staring at me, he lets out a long-suffering sigh. "It's too late, Rhy—for you, anyway."

I brace for another fight, but he launches straight into the air and leaves me behind. The hollowness that follows nearly drops me to my knees.

Vikarus is my twin, my other half. How can he just leave me and pretend I'm not his brother?

Why does he have to be so stubborn?

Slecking hell.

CHAPTER TWENTY-TWO

Creed

The world erupts in a cacophony of weapons fire, growls, and the kind of screams that cut off with a finality that makes me shudder. Calli and the phoenix quint are brutally formidable, and I realize that when they ended our little first contact siege when the rift first opened they really did kick our asses because they honestly didn't even break a sweat.

How is she? Keyla asks racing along beside me, her nose in the air as she scents for danger.

Hawk and Lukas are leading the way back to the trucks, Kotah and Jaxx have caught up to us, the bears are right behind us, Calli's still holding off the reinforcements, and I have no idea where Rhy disappeared to.

I saw him and Vik toppling through the sky and then they were gone. Thankfully, even as angry as he probably is, I don't think Vik will hurt him.

Creed? Are you all right?

I swallow and get my head back into the moment at hand. *Yes, apologies. She's still unconscious, but I sense the strength of her mental energy. I think they simply induced some kind of coma to keep her locked down.*

I'm sure between Calli's tears, Doc, and Jaxx, she'll be up and around in no time.

That's my mate. Forever a budding flower blooming optimism.

"Hello, Creed." The greeting comes from behind a broad tree to my left and Laryssa steps into view.

She's looking paler than usual and I chuckle at the silk-wrapped nub at the end of her arm. "I like the new accessorizing. You should consider going stump with both arms."

"Don't be rude. It's beneath you."

I chuckle. "You don't know a fucking thing about me, Laryssa. You never did."

"I know you think you're getting out of here with your sister."

"Because I am."

"Did you forget I own you two?"

"Not anymore you don't, bitch." I turn to Lukas and Hawk and meet the men eye-to-eye. "Get her to the truck and get her free of this place. Whatever happens to me, it'll be worth it if I know she's safe."

Lukas shakes his head. "Jaxx, you're up. You've got Honor. I've got the witch."

The jaguar shifts in an instant and takes my sister over his shoulder. Hawk positions himself to take on any incoming hostiles. "We'll secure her and double back to help."

"No. Just go. Keyla, you go too."

Yeah right. Not bloody likely. If this is the showdown, I'm not missing the fight.

There's no sense arguing—no time either. Me handing off my sister isn't well received and the blood witch launches into an attack.

I've been taken down by her before and know how powerful

she is, so it surprises the hell out of me when the shooting streams of magic bounce off an invisible barrier and do us no harm.

"Nicely done, Lukas," Rhylan says, shifting as he lands behind me.

Laryssa's lip curls as she focuses on the dragon. "I was hoping you bled out."

"Same," he says. "Nice stump. I think you should go for a matching pair."

I laugh. "I just said that."

Laryssa screeches and the path breaks out in a riot of fighting. The blood witch tries to aid Laryssa in taking us down but Lukas is negating the witch's power. It's a stalemate until something inside me starts to burn.

Dropping to my knees, I fight the demon beast inside me. I lose so much of myself when I become that thing. My will is not my own and I can't risk the witch turning me against my family.

I'd rather die first.

Creed? What's wrong? What's happening?

The witch... she's calling the curse. I can't control the beast. I fall to all fours, panting and fighting the pull of my dark soul. The breaking of bones and the tearing of tendons have me gritting my teeth. As always, I'm lost to the pain of the shift. *Stop me, Little Wolf. Knock me out or put me down but don't let me kill any of you.*

Keyla

I hear the desperation in Creed's plea and search for a way to end his suffering. How do I knock out a man twice my size with far more power than I even know about?

No. The answer doesn't lay with me taking him out. It's

Laryssa and the witch that need to meet their end. I reach out to Rhylan and Doc and find the mental communication we share. *The witch is calling Creed's beast to take us out. We need to take her and Laryssa out first.*

I'm no help, Rhylan says. *I've been rigged with a safety protocol. As much as I want to, I can't kill them.*

Okay, then you take care of your brother and leave them to us.

My brother?

I glance toward the sky to where Vikarus is descending fast. *He brought friends.*

Rhylan follows my gaze and lets off a string of curses. *He brought the enforcers of my brood. He must've gone to Shadowcaster and turned me in as a traitor. This just went from bad to worse.*

Anyone got a backup army we could call? Doc asks.

Creed and Honor do. The Amberloq are their guardian warriors. Creed called on their power before and used it to break the bonds of the blood witch.

Do you think he could do it again? Rhy asks.

I honestly don't know. Cover my butt. I'm going to try something. I shift back and drop to my knees in front of a writhing Creed. Gripping his head in my hands, I try to remember the sensation of what it felt like when Creed called to the ancient power of the Amberloq.

Sitting in the center of the dirt path, I close my eyes and focus on the arcane power of the Thornebane ancestors. It's part of me now. Not fully, but since the searing, I've felt Creed's heritage power build in my cells.

The effects of the witch's curse are crippling. Connected as we are, I feel the excruciating agony as Creed breaks apart from the inside. His shift isn't like mine. His is a violation and unwanted abomination that works to consume him more with each shift.

I lock my shoulders and send him what comfort I can. *Creed, focus on me. Help me call your guardians for help.*

The horrible images of the mental and physical abuse he's suffered begin to slow as my prince fights to connect. My wolf lets off a long, baleful cry, sickened by the haunting devastation our love is infected with each time he fights the queen's hold.

Connect with the Amberloq. Help me call on their powers to break you free from the witch's hold.

The loop of horror-filled images slows even more. Creed's father having his throat ripped out, his mother stripped and thrown down a stone staircase, Honor being assaulted after he tried to escape, Bloom, bleeding and dying on the ground before him.

Stay with me, my prince. Focus on the power you need to break free from this. I know you can do this. I know we can do this.

I startle as an influx of power bursts to life in the back of my mind. It's bright and powerful and it builds with a ferocity and sureness that is both overwhelming and invigorating. My heart races triple-time as the power of many minds floods forward, it is raw mental energy and exactly the power boost Creed needs.

Pressing my forehead to his, I hope he's receiving this gift as much as I am. I think he is.

His tremors have stopped and his fight to not shift into the demon wolf is won.

Following the web of golden pathways, I probe his mind and find the black and scarlet rope binding his will from being his own.

I know this is the witch's tether and I focus all my strength on snapping that rope... unraveling it... untying it. I don't care how it ceases being attached as long as it does. I won't have Creed suffering under their control anymore. Their influence ends now.

Pushing all the healing strength I possess into my mate, I banish every trace of those two bitches.

Creed is mine: body, mind, and soul. *Mine.*

Doc

I'm not sure what Keyla is doing, but it's something big. The hair on my entire body is standing on end and the two of them are glowing with this wild, golden aura.

As scary as it is to see, it's also beautiful.

I always knew Keyla was greatness waiting to be unleashed on the world and the universe seems to agree.

Brant and Kotah are with me, guarding the two of them and I wonder if Rhylan sees what's happening.

I cast a glance skyward and struggle to draw breath. Rhy and Calli are battling the aerial attack while we take on the ground forces.

Lukas is a freaking phenom.

There's another person who is spectacular waiting to be recognized. Every spell the blood witch throws out, Lukas counters. Every attack she makes, he sends it back at her three-fold.

The queen is looking mighty nervous.

What's the matter, bitch, afraid you might have to fight a battle yourself?

Yeah, I get the feeling that she's more of a slimy behind-the-scenes plotter, not an adversary of honor to be reckoned with. Well, the tides have turned, and I think she's starting to realize it.

Creed pushes up onto his feet and helps Keyla stand beside him. They're still glowing gold and honestly, there is energy ebbing off them.

I catch the look of fear on Laryssa's face as Creed stands to his full height. "You're done, Laryssa."

She offers him a forced smile and shakes her head. "You can't harm me. I made sure of that."

"But I can," Keyla raises her arm, and a steady stream of magic pulses out of the mating tattoo on her palm. Both Laryssa and the scarlet witch stiffen and are thrown to the ground. "I wish upon you only that which you inflicted upon Creed. Feel the pain and torment you caused him and bear his suffering."

The two women are writhing in the dirt, screaming as the onslaught of Keyla's torture takes hold.

"Consider yourself overthrown, Laryssa," Creed says, grinning. "Go back to whatever rock you crawled out from under and die there." He bends down, kisses Keyla, and then looks up at the sky. "Enough."

With the swipe of one hand through the air, half a dozen dragons let off a scream and retreat.

Rhylan and Calli land a moment later and other than some cuts and Calli having a bleeding nose, they don't look too bad.

Rhy joins Creed, Keyla, and me, and gestures to the two of them throwing off luminescence. "This is a new look. Very royal and shiny."

Creed holds up his hands. "It's Keyla's doing. I'm not sure what she did, but all the intricate connections I used to have to the Amberloq have been restored. I'm powering up more by the minute."

Rhylan hugs Creed and slaps his back. "Congratulations. I honestly couldn't be happier for you."

"She also took care of those two," I say, pointing to Laryssa and— "Where the fuck is the witch?"

Keyla and Calli and I scan the area and frown.

Lukas wipes his face with the sleeve of his shirt. "She portaled out somehow. When the going gets tough the witch gets going."

"Damn it."

"They both deserve to die," Rhylan says.

Lukas nods. "They will. For tonight, overthrowing Laryssa will have to do."

Rhy nods. "If I could do it myself, I would. My father always said you need to end your enemies. You don't leave a mangy dog feral in your backyard."

"No, you don't." Lukas pulls his gun from his holster and tilts his head toward Calli and Keyla. "Why don't you boys take your ladies to the trucks and check on your sister. I'll take care of things here and be right behind you."

"Yeah," Creed says, giving us each a once-over. "I'm done here. Let's get Honor home and reclaim our lives and my throne."

I wrap my arm around Keyla's shoulder and Brant does the same with Calli. "Best idea I've heard in ages."

Keyla smiles up at me and then extends her tattooed hand out to Creed. The moment their palms meet, the tension of the night drains away. "We've got some exciting days ahead of us."

Rhy bends at the waist and gestures with a sweeping hand toward the path. "Lead the way, King Creed."

~~ THE END ~~

Thank you for reading Dark Soul the Seventh book in the Guardian's of the Fae Realms series and book two of Keyla's harem.
Claim book 8 – Dark Crown now.
If you are inclined to help a girl out, it would be amazing if you could leave a star rating or review.
If you want more, join my newsletter and be notified when new books launch and for all my news and sales!

Author Notes

Written on 04/26/2021

It's great to be back with the Guardians of the Fae Realms again and turning up the heat on my storytelling. For those of you who don't know, I write my sexy/steamy urban fantasy, paranormal, and sci-fi romance as JL Madore and my 'no sex' novels for the same genres but just closed door under the name Auburn Tempest. That pen name has had a great run lately with the Chronicles of an Urban Druid series and I focused on getting a book a month out in that series for three months.

It took me away from RH for a bit, but I'm happy to be back.

So, thank you for reading and continuing to spend time with Calli and Keyla and the men they can't help but love. There's plenty coming at Creed and Keyla and Doc's going to be right there with them putting it all together.

Hugs to all,

JL

ALSO BY JL MADORE

Find Me:

My Direct Sales Site: Shopify

Social Media – Facebook, X, Instagram, tiktok

Web page – www.jlmadore.com

Dauntless Publishing Inc. (Our family business)

Email – jlmadorewrites@gmail.com

Discord— https://discord.gg/uwgngKeF3a

Reader Group – JL Series Updates

For a complete and up to date list of works, please visit JL Madore's
author page at www.dauntlesspub.com/jl-madore

Diamond Dagger Mafia

Book 1 - Siege of Blood and Betrayal

Book 2 - Clash of Sin and Secret

JL's Reverse Harem Titles

Guardians of the Fae Realms

Guardians of the Phoenix – Calli's Harem

Book 1 – Rise of the Phoenix

Book 2 – Wolf's Soul

Book 3 – Bear's Strength

Book 4 – Hawk's Heart

Book 5 – Jaguar's Passion

Darkness Calls – Keyla's harem

Book 6 – Dark Curse

Book 7 – Dark Soul

Book 8 – Dark Crown

Guardians of the Crown – Honor's Harem

Book 9 – Honor Restored

Book 10 – Honor Guards

Book 11 – Honor Bound

Book 12 – Honor Empowered

Rise of the Amberloq – Lark's Harem

Book 13 – Find the Fallen

Book 14 – Rise from Ruin

Book 15 – Trust and Triumph

Exemplar Hall

Exemplar Hall – Jesse's Harem

Book 1 – Captured by the Magi

Book 2 – Jesse and the Magi Vault

Book 3 – The Makings of a Magi Knight

Book 4 – Clash with the Magi Council

Book 5 – The Unstoppable Storme

Club Sanguine

Book 1 – Moonstone Maelstrom

Book 2 - Sunstone Sacrifice

Book 3 – Witchstone Warrior

JL's More Traditional M/F, M/M, or Menage

The Watchers of the Gray Series (Paranormal)

Book 1 – Watcher Untethered – Zander

Book 2 – Watcher Redeemed – Kyrian

Book 3 – Watcher Reborn – Danel

Book 4 – Watcher Divided – Phoenix

Book 5 – Watcher United – Seth

Book 6 – Watcher Compelled – Bo

Book 7 – Watcher Unfeigned – Brennus

Book 8 – Watcher Exposed – Taharqa

The Scourge Survivor Series (Fantasy)

Book 1 – Blaze Ignites

Book 2 – Ursa Unearthed

Book 3 – Torrent of Tears

Book 4 – Blind Spirit

Book 5 – Fate's Journey

Book 6 – Savage Love – epilogue novella

Aliens of Atlantis Series (Sci-Fi)

Book 1 – Taryn's Tiderider

Book 2 – Kai's Captive

Book 3 – Alyandra's Shadow